Evasion

Mark Leslie

Stark Publishing

Hamilton, Ontario

Stark Publishing
Hamilton, Ontario
www.markleslie.ca

Book Layout © 2014 BookDesignTemplates.com

Evasion / Mark Leslie -- 1st ed.
ISBN 978-0-9735688-5-1

For Dad

It doesn't matter who my father was; it matters who I remember he was.

—ANNE SEXTON

Contents

Author's Note

This novella was inspired by a phenomenon that kept happening shortly after my father died unexpectedly on an operating room table.

I kept spotting him everywhere: In the car driving beside me on the highway, in the stands of a hockey stadium and even across the tracks at a train station. I knew it was my imagination -- but, I speculated -- what if it wasn't in my head?

What if it actually **was** him?

What if he was still alive, unbeknownst to all his loved ones?

The concept wouldn't leave - but it kept becoming more than a short story but not quite a full length novel, so I kept putting it aside until November 2013 when, committing to write 50,000 words for NaNoWriMo (National Novel Writing Month), I let the ideas that had been swirling inside my mind come out.

And the result is a Die-Hard styled quick paced thriller that I have had a lot of fun with and that readers have told me they would like to see more of.

If you like this, please consider leaving a review wherever you read it or on your favorite online review website. Feel free to email me at mark@markleslie.ca to let me know what you thought

Mark Leslie
June 2014

Prologue

Scott Desmond was looking at a dead man.

He shook his head, swiped at the sweat running down his forehead and into his eyes, tried to focus more clearly on the sight before him.

There was no mistake about it.

The man he was looking at across two sets of train tracks was none other than his father – a man who had died almost eighteen months earlier.

Scott shook his head for the second time, rubbed his eyes, tried to focus through the humidity of the August day. But there was simply no disputing the fact.

The man he was staring at across the GO train platform *had* to be his father.

The man had first caught his attention because of the unique way he walked. The man, in his early-sixties, moved with a distinct lurching gait. He shuffled forward, half-dragging, half-lifting his partially crippled left leg; a movement Scott was intimately familiar with.

From his earliest memories, Scott both visually and audibly recognized his father's unique way of getting about. The man, whom, Scott had learned, had almost lost his life at the age of twenty-one in a spectacular motorcycle accident on the highway, ended up walking away from the crash with a single side-effect.

Perhaps calling the response "walking away" was a bit of an exaggeration. It was only after a series of three intense surgeries and almost two full years of intense therapy that Lionel Desmond was able to walk, and at that, in the lurching gait that Scotty came to associate specifically with his father.

For example, his father, an early riser, would get up and proceed down the hallway to the kitchen to put on the coffee, and Scotty, lying in bed, could hear the unique step and slide movement his father made. Years later, he could instantly spot his father in the hallways of the school where he worked as a custodian, and could tell, even from a few dozen yards away, that the man moving in a half-step, half dragging walk, one in which the man's left leg dragged along, in a lurching drag-step motion that was immediately distinct and unique.

That step, that unique lurching gait, was what first caught Scott's attention when he was standing on the GO train platform and waiting for the train that would take him back home from Exhibition Station to Hamilton.

His father had died, suddenly, one bitter cold morning in February nearly two years earlier.

He had been diagnosed with a cyst on his liver; a lump that the doctors weren't exactly sure was benign or malevolent. But the best option, the doctors had agreed (both Lionel's family doctor and the specialist who had been assigned to his case), was to have the preventative surgery to remove the kidney, in hope of nipping the cancer in the bud.

After a brief family discussion, which was easy enough to do, considering Scott was the only son of Lionel and Jeannette Desmond, it was decided that Lionel would undergo the surgery, have the cyst and entire kidney removed, and be able to move on to enjoying the imminent retirement that lay less than six months before him. Only, the day of the surgery led to a strange combination of delays and angst. Scotty had driven back to his home town in Parry Sound, Ontario from his home in Hamilton to be a part of it all, be the self-appointed chauffeur for his parents during this ordeal. And, needing to be at the Sudbury hospital for 8:00 AM in order to be ready for the 9:00 AM scheduled surgery, they had had to leave Parry sound a few minutes after 6:00 AM. So they had already been up for an extended period of time and anxiously awaiting the impending surgery, when hospital staff kept returning to the pre-op room they had all been waiting in to inform them that the surgery was, again, delayed for another hour.

And so, with a surgery scheduled for 10:00 AM which continued to be pushed back until just a few minutes shy of noon, everybody had been exhausted and frustrated.

That hadn't prevented Scott's father from turning on his trademark charm, however. Despite the waiting and the angst and frustration, Lionel Desmond continued to make small talk and crack silly jokes with the hospital staff who continued to flit in and out of the waiting room.

"Know what we're having for dinner?" Lionel would quip. "Steak and kidney pie!"

The hospital staff would cast a confused look at him – most of them didn't realize that Lionel was awaiting surgery to have his kidney removed. But Scott and his mother rolled their eyes and groaned audibly every time he tossed that chestnut out to a new staff member who arrived to deliver the bad news that the surgeon was running behind and Lionel's surgery would again be delayed.

Despite the older gentleman's good humor, Scott had been frustrated.

His original thought was that he would be at the hospital for the morning and then could move on to an appointment he had scheduled for lunch time; but the delays in surgery put his entire schedule in jeopardy. Though he loved his father, there was a stream of frustration and anger flowing through him as he thought about the client who would be waiting for him.

All that frustration and angst, of course, fled him less than two hours later when his mother called him on his mobile phone.

Scott had been at a diner in downtown Sudbury, just about to close a deal with the client he had been forced to delay for more than two hours when his cell phone had rang. He looked down to see who it was, and noticed it was his mother. She had stayed behind at the hospital to wait until the surgery was over. Scott had planned on returning after his meeting to take them both back home.

"Scott. It's Mom." Her words were short, each one punching a hole in the air.

"What is it?"

"It's Dad," she said, and then tried to say something more, but she couldn't force the words through. She began to cry.

His father had died in the recovery room. He had just been coming to, according to hospital staff, and even beginning to mumble the jokes they had already come to expect from him; then he dropped off, dying from internal bleeding when the clips on his renal artery came off.

That had been eighteen months ago. And despite the anger, the rallying against the institution and never getting any answers, a long and painful, tiring haul, it still seemed like yesterday.

So when Scott noticed the man on across the tracks, lumbering down the platform, he called out in a loud voice: "Dad!"

That's when the man turned and looked directly into his eyes.

There was simply no mistaking it. It was his father.

His father looked him directly in the eyes.

The man's eyes were filled with recognition and something Scott had never seen in them before.

Terror.

Utter, outright terror.

"Dad!" he called again, this time in a louder voice.

Oh my God! It's Dad. He's alive. And he's right over there! The voice ran through Scott's head and he looked toward the entrance that led to the underground path that would take him under the tracks and over to his father's side. Then he looked back at his father.

That's when the train pulled in to the station, blocking his father off from his view.

Shocked at the thought of being cut off from being able to see his Dad, Scott stood there a moment, the impossibility of it all rushing through his mind.

Dad, he thought. *It's Dad. He can't possibly be standing there. But there he is. He's alive.*

He stood there a minute longer, trying to tell himself that he had been seeing things.

"But I'm not," Scott said. "I'm not seeing things." That walk, that lurching gait. And he stared the man in the eyes. As sure as Scott was standing on the train platform, that had been his father standing right across from him.

As the train came to a complete stop, Scott realized his father had been planning on getting on the train. The horrified look on his face told him he wouldn't be waiting around.

Scott knew he had to get over there. Now.

He sprinted down the platform towards the shelter that led to the stairs, moving so quickly that he ran right into the door as a man in a business suit was opening it.

"Watch it!" the man yelled as the door pushed back against him.

Scott shuffled around the door, danced around the man without saying a word and ran inside towards the stairs. He raced up the stairs two at a time, barely missing an older woman who was slowly making her way with one hand on the rail and the other clutching a walker.

"Oh my goodness!" the woman yelled, beginning to lose her balance. Scott spotted it happening and was able to pause, take a step back and place a hand on the small of her back to steady her back to her feet.

"Sorry ma'am," Scott said,

"You young people are always in such a rush," the woman scolded. "Look what you almost did."

"So sorry ma'am," Scott kept his hand on her back and helped her move up the stairs.

"If you gave yourself time and planned ahead, you wouldn't be late and rushing around to catch your train."

"Yes ma'am. Sorry ma'am. Goodbye, ma'am."

Scott then turned, leaped down the stairs, turned right and raced through the tunnel. His footsteps echoed off the tiled walls along with the repeated calls of "Dad!" which he yelled as he ran.

At the base of the stairs going up Scott stepped in a slick puddle of spilled soft drink and slid into the bottom step. His left toe caught on the bottom riser and he tumbled forward, his left shin and left forearm taking most of the brunt of his fall as he came down on the stairs.

"Dammit!" he yelled as intense bursts of pain flashed through his leg and arm. The shin took the worst of the pain and throbbed painfully as he tried to pull himself into a crawling position. He could hear that the train hadn't yet left; there was a muffled announcement being broadcast about it, but he couldn't hear it because there was somebody standing over him and talking to him.

"Are you okay, man?" a young man in a rainbow-colored poncho asked, placing a hand on Scott's shoulder.

"Fine," Scott said. "I'm fine!" And he groaned as he got to his feet, the shin sending out protesting throbs of pain.

He hobbled up the stairs and slowly managed to push past the pain, to keep walking.

At the top of the stairs, he found it slightly quicker going on flat ground and limped out the entrance, turning right to head back toward the platform, his leg continued to scream in protest as he moved.

He was less than forty feet from the train when he saw the doors closing.

"No!" he screamed.

He raced to the spot on the platform where he had seen his father standing.

His father was not there. Obviously, he was on the train. As Scott got to the spot where his father had been standing just minutes earlier, the train started to pass and he caught his father's eyes, yet again, through the window of the train, looking right at him.

That same look of recognition mingled with an aura of terror was on the man's face.

"Dad!" Scott screamed, over and over as the train pulled his father out of his life yet again. "Dad! Dad! Daaaaaaad!"

Chapter One

Today

The last thing Scotty Desmond expected, when standing in the doorway to Herb Canter's office, was the pistol his boss held pointed at his face.

Scott had been called into Herb's office just a few minutes earlier; Herb Canter, Digi-Life's Director of Infrastructure Technology, was, essentially Scott's boss – or at least as close to a boss as Scott had had in the past half dozen years. Scott Desmond was an independent contractor, an IT consultant who specialized in helping companies find and fix potential security holes in their systems.

Digi-Life was an online insurance company, a start-up self-service provider of various insurance options available, from life insurance to car and home insurance, linking up both small and multinational insurance firms with clients world-wide.

Scotty's past as a freelance hacker lent him the knowledge, skill, and expertise to be able to find even the most innocuous gaps, holes, and gateways that hackers could use to gain access to a company's system and critical data. He charged a significant fee for his services and time, and found that, despite his initial reservations about the change in lifestyle – moving from a life of well-paying crime to a life of helping others and being employed through legal means – the consultant work did bring him a significant income.

He had been working with Digi-Life for the past six months and quite enjoyed the consistency of returning to a regular office. It was satisfying to return to a workplace on such a regular basis that he knew at least a couple of dozen people by name; enough to even enjoy going out for beers with a few of his co-workers.

And, until the morning that he pointed a pistol at Scotty's head, Herb Canter had been a decent enough boss, someone Scott actually felt comfortable working with and even respected.

Scott had been taking a break from the hack routine he was using to QA test a new security gateway that Digi-Life was hoping to implement, and, taking a short morning coffee-break, was fiddling on the mini laptop he kept in a small backpack near him at all times. Though he had abandoned his previous life of corrupt hacking for nefarious purposes, there was one side-project he kept pecking away at. He was exploring the files and reports associated with his father's death almost five years earlier.

Requesting official documents from the hospital, the provincial Coroner's office and even via CSIS had resulted in road-blocks, denied access and subterfuge. The only way Scott had been able to gain any insights was through hacking into the private and locked records that had been kept from his eyes.

It was a painstaking process, but something he was committed to not give up on. He had, after all, seen his father, who had supposedly died on an operating room table, walking around, alive and well at a train station just down the street from where Scott was now working. There seemed to be deeper layers of conflicting information associated with his father's supposed death. And the further he dug, the more confused and intrigued he'd become.

Virtually every free moment he was not working was dedicated to this side project, this special investigation that continued to slowly reveal intriguing details. He always conducted that work from his personal mini laptop, the one he had a direct masked Wi-Fi hotspot through, rather than the laptop his employer had assigned him. He kept the mini laptop, the backpack he hauled it and a series of special hacker tools and equipment around in, at all times.

Lately, despite having followed many dead-end paths, Scott seemed to be getting somewhere. Just a couple of weeks earlier he had uncovered a previously unearthed revelation about one of the doctors who had been in his father's hospital room, and was potentially on his way to figuring out how it might be possible for his father, supposedly dead, to be walking around. Scott felt very close to being able to locate this particular doctor, and knew, that it was just a matter of time before he'd get to him and get an answer.

So when Herb sent Scott a text message on his mobile phone requesting that Scott pop in to see him, Scott immediately snapped shut the laptop and slid it into the backpack before walking down the hall to the man's office, just as naturally and effortlessly as he would have picked a coffee mug from a kitchen cupboard and poured himself a drink.

Herb was a decent boss and the perfect one in Scott's opinion. He was smart enough to understand the intricacies of what he was asking Scott to do, and also knowledgeable enough about what he didn't understand, and could leave in Scott's capable hands.

Scott respected that, and the man. Though he worked freelance, Herb Canter was the type of boss Scott could see himself working for full time. He kept just enough distance to allow people to get their jobs done, and seemed to have the special knack for stepping in to assist and support at just the right time.

So when Scott pushed Herb's office door opened to find the man sitting at his desk, a small black pistol pointed at Scott's head, he was more than a little surprised.

"Herb, what's going on?" Scott said, starting down the muzzle of the weapon.

"Step inside and close the door," Herb said.

"I don't --"

"Close the door!" Herb repeated.

Scott noticed that the man's eyes had a unique glazed quality. His eyes were focused and intelligent, just like they had always been, but there was an additional layer of something almost indistinguishable masking his face; something Scott could only think of as a slightly glazed look – almost as if Herb were looking at Scott through an additional think gauze or filter.

"Okay," Scott said, turning to close the door. "Just give me a second here..."

A small hole punching into the drywall beside Scott's head startled him; a split second later a sound like a metal ruler slapped down hard onto his desk filled the room. Scott ducked down to the floor, realizing Herb had taken a shot at his head and missed by a mere inch or two.

"Herb? What the fuck?" Scott yelled, scrambling on the floor and out the doorway. Out of the corner of his eye he spotted the black handgun with the incredibly long pistol barrel – a silencer? – in Herb's hand.

"You won't get away!" Herb yelled after him in a deep monotone voice. "You cannot evade us!"

Scott crab-crawled around the corner of the office entrance before getting to his feet and sprinting toward the exit, his backpack still atop of his left shoulder. Ahead, he spotted one of the company's security guards walking quickly from the fourth floor stairwell entrance, his eyes fixed on Scott.

"Hurry!" Scott yelled, pointing over his shoulder. "I don't know what's going on, but Herb has a gun and he's shooting!"

The guard didn't say anything, but his eyes remained locked on Scott.

Even from thirty feet away, there was something eerily familiar about the glassy-eyed glaze in the man's eyes as he reached to his belt to draw a weapon.

"Oh shit," Scott said, stopping in his tracks.

Scott knew that Digi-Life security guards didn't carry firearms, but they did carry mag lites, and at least one of them had Tasers. He wasn't sure what this one was carrying, but, even if he couldn't clearly read the intent in the man's glazed eyes, it came through quite distinctly in his words.

"You won't get away!" The guard said, in the same monotone voice Herb had previously used. "You cannot evade us!"

Chapter Two

Four-and-a-half Years Ago

Scotty spent most of the morning that his father died with his nose buried in a book.

The rest of the time, he had mostly been anxious about an appointment that had been scheduled.

He had, of course, driven to Parry Sound to spend the previous day with his parents and be there in the wee morning hours to drive them up in to the city for Lionel Desmond's early morning surgery, but, at the time he had felt as if he were a mere assistant to the whole procedure.

Sure, the surgery had been a serious one – the removal of a kidney with a potentially malignant cyst on it – but explained by the doctors as routine enough that Lionel Desmond might perhaps be going in for a tonsillectomy rather than a nephrectomy.

It wasn't quite day surgery, but it was one in which the man would, after being observed overnight in hospital, be allowed to return home the next day.

So, the dutiful son – although he had, at first been reluctant to play that role – Scotty took the trek north from Toronto to his parent's home. At least, he told himself he was a dutiful son; and his parents fully believed he was being a dutiful son.

What he didn't tell them was that, conveniently, he had hooked up with a potential client online; and, though Scotty was there to play the role of helpful and dutiful son, it had been the lucrative nature of meeting with the client and taking on a new job that had appealed to him most.

Sure, he loved his father; but this was a potential huge cash windfall that he simply couldn't ignore.

Scotty was a seasoned and sought-after hacker.

He had been adept with computers since the very first day that his father brought the computer home from the high school where he worked. It had been a Commodore Pet Computer, among the first "home computers" to be wide distributed and used in various mid-northern high schools across the province.

Scotty had relished in seeing that a simple series of words written in a particular order in a certain format – in this case, the programming language being BASIC with each line of code, a logical statement telling the computer an action to perform denoted in numeral order – you could get this machine to do things.

The first program that had sparked Scotty's imagination was when the teacher had instructed them how to have the computer flash the word "HELLO" to them over and over.

```
10 PRINT "HELLO!"
20 PAUSE 1
30 CLS
40 PAUSE 1
50 GOTO 10
```

When you ran the program, it would display the characters "HELLO!" on an otherwise blank screen – a series of green letters on a black screen – then a timer would count out exactly one second, then clear the screen, count out another second, then return to the first line of the program and repeat the process. The result, a flashing "HELLO!" of green letters in the top left hand corner of the otherwise blank black computer screen

The original instructions had been to just type in "HELLO!" but Scotty had figured out he could insert virtually any characters in there, so immediately changed that to "HELLO SCOTTY!"

As his classmates were fooling around with just getting that simple five lines of code to work, Scotty found himself immediately bored and tried to use the basic understanding to create something a little bit more complex.

So he modified it to the following:

```
10 PRINT "HELLO SCOTTY!"
20 PAUSE 3
30 CLS
40 PRINT "HAVE A GREAT DAY . . ."
50 PAUSE 1
60 CLS
70 PRINT ". . . BUTTHEAD!"
80 PAUSE 5
90 CLS
100 PAUSE 2
110 GOTO 10
```

This particular program printed "HELLO SCOTTY!" then cleared the screen, then the words "HAVE A GREAT DAY . . ." appeared, then the screen cleared again, then ". . . BUTTHEAD!" appeared, before the routine would repeat.

It had, essentially, been Scotty's first "hack" – taking an existing program, understanding how it worked and then manipulating it to do something that he wanted, rather than the original intention of the teacher!

And, of course, being satisfied with the result, but wanting to experiment with what else he could do, he tweaked the code to remove the final "clear screen" prompt – he changed the program to the following:

```
10 PRINT "HELLO SCOTTY!"
20 PAUSE 2
30 CLS
40 PRINT "HAVE A GREAT DAY . . ."
50 PAUSE 2
60 CLS
70 PRINT ". . . BUTTHEAD!"
100 PAUSE 5
110 GOTO 70
```

By removing lines eighty and ninety he had learned that the code was numeral in nature and didn't need to follow a particular pattern – he could skip or insert numbers – so long as they were in numerical order they worked fine. This meant he could insert nine statements between any of the existing lines.

He also determined that by clearing the final "clear screen message" and not returning back to the original first line, he could alter the manner by which the program worked. By returning the statement that allowed him to print ". . . BUTTHEAD!" on the screen repeatedly, the program ran through the original statement, the second one, and then the punch line, which repeated.

It was a rudimentary hack of the original program being taught, but it kept Scotty enthusiastic about what else could be done.

"Cool!" the student beside Scotty had said when he saw Scotty running the program beside him.

A few other students at the desk beside him looked and started laughing, asking him to break the program and repeat it again.

Then the teacher, Mr. Prescott, came over – and this had likely been the determining factor that meant embracing computer programming or forgetting about it as one of the simple experiments children do when learning something new in school.

Mr. Prescott had originally frowned, in that manner that teachers had to frown upon witnessing students behaving out of the expected order of things – but then a wry grin crossed his face and he stood there nodding, his red hair and red beard bobbing and swaying slightly behind the movements of his head.

"I see you have grasped the rudimentary elements of BASIC, Mister Desmond," Mr. Prescott said.

"Yes, sir," Scotty said, looking down at his desk, unable to meet the teacher's eyes.

"That's not what I had instructed you to do, is it?"

"No, sir,"

"When the bell rings for lunch, you will stay here and help me tidy the computer lab for my afternoon class."

"Yes, sir."

Scotty sighed a bit of relief. He hadn't been sent to the principal's office; nor had this landed him detention. Cleaning the lab for a few minutes after everyone else had been dismissed was a relatively easy punishment.

So when the bell did ring fifteen minutes later and Scotty stayed behind, he learned he wasn't being held back for punishment, but rather, for extra work. Interesting work.

"You're pretty adept at using the computer," Mr. Prescott said to him just a second after the last student left the class, casting a weary glance back at Scotty as she walked out. The teacher's elbows were on the table and he had tented his hands together, stroking the underside of his red beard with his two intertwined index fingers.

"Yes, sir,"

"The program you wrote was juvenile in nature."

"Yes, sir,"

"But you can do better," Prescott said, putting his hands down on the desk and pushing himself up to his feet, an intriguing glimmering spark in his eyes. "Much better! You have an undeniable talent, and I think it would be worth your time to continue to explore this, to work at it. Are you willing to work at it? Are you willing to work hard at learning more?"

Scotty was confused. Mr. Prescott seemed excited. He had been expecting him to ask if he was willing to be better, not act in a juvenile fashion.

"Uh, yes, sir!"

"Excellent! Computers are going to be an integral part of our future, Mister Desmond. If you embrace them now, learn all you can, the world will be yours!"

Scotty and Mr. Prescott never left the computer lab for the entire lunch period – Prescott walked him through even more programming language options, complex routines, taught him additional commands and programs and, by the end of the day, Scotty was marveling at how easy it was to create stick figure animations on the screen.

The next day, Mr. Prescott taught him more about the wonder of what he could do using BASIC programming language. He took the boy under his wing and showed him the amazing possibilities that lay before him. By the end of the month, after a series of ongoing personalized tutorial sessions at least every second day, Scotty's skill at programming in BASIC ended up surpassing his mentor's own ability. Scotty started teaching his master new tricks, new options.

"You've got a real gift for this," Mr. Prescott bemused one late afternoon when they had been working together in the computer lab after school. Despite the fact Scotty had moved well beyond his mentor's skill level, he still fed off of the encouragement, praise and guidance the middle-aged man provided. And Prescott's unwavering belief in Scotty, his willingness to push him harder, to help him achieve higher levels of skill, helped feed Scotty's confidence, his self-worth – all at a time when that was one of the most important things to develop in a young teenager's mind and heart.

"Thank you," Scotty said in return, a proud smile erupting onto his face.

"No, my young friend," Prescott replied. "Thank YOU!"

And that ongoing relationship, of course, led to Scotty's real passion. When the Commodore Pet was replaced by the Commodore 128, and, simultaneously, when Scotty's parents purchased the Commodore VIC-20 for the home, he continued to practice his BASIC programming skills; then moved on to PASCAL. He watched the television show *Bits and Bytes* featuring Billy Van and Luba Goy, knowing virtually as much as the show's host (Van) and his computer-connected mentor (Goy), but still marveling at the wonder of computers.

Prescott also introduced him to various computer magazines, such as *Computer & Video Games* and *Compute!* and Scotty reveled in the monthly columns and articles by programmers sharing their programs, which would be typed out in long form for avid readers of the magazine to key into their own computers to try out on their own. Scotty, of course, tried them all, and often experimented with adapting their codes into his own. He even submitted a few of his own adapted codes to the magazine after some encouragement from Mr. Prescott.

Which led to Scotty actually writing a monthly column for *Computer Programmers Monthly*, one of the many magazines Scotty ended up subscribing to. Scotty used a pen name for these articles, and Mr. Prescott submitted them on his behalf.

Scotty wrote these articles under the name Commandor (a word that combined Commander and Commadore) Mr. Prescott handled all of the submission of material, including cashing the checks and ensuring Scotty received his payment. Scotty kept this alter ego to himself – or between his mentor and himself – it was almost like a superhero secret identity. Scotty quite liked the idea of having an ability, a "super power" so to speak, that nobody else knew about. Mr. Prescott was like Scott's own personal superhero buddy, mentor and support system, a combination of Mister Miyagi from the Karate Kid movies and Alfred, Batman's personal servant.

Throughout the years, even when he moved off to University and seldom saw Mr. Prescott – who retired the same year Scotty graduated from university – the secret identity was something only the two of them shared.

That had been the start of Scotty's pseudonym, or what became his hacker name. The magazine only lasted about four years before being replaced, but there had been enough of an underground community of hackers, and, as bulletin board systems, the precursors to the internet, came on the scene in mid-to-late 1980s and early 1990s, Scotty found a whole new group of anonymous colleagues who were part of the hacker scene.

As the bulletin boards eventually gave way to the Freenets and other online communities that became the Internet and World-Wide Web, Scotty, as Commandor became a well-known hacker.

Though he maintained a regular career as a talented computer programmer, Scotty kept up his secret hacker identity. Which eventually led to the hacker lifestyle, which led to lucrative jobs, and being able to choose which of the many opportunities that were offered to him, such as the one that drew him to Sudbury.

After years of working in IT, Scotty had a sideline of business in which he would work on various hacks, both personal and professional; the demand for his skills became so huge that he had at first dropped down to part time and took on some tasks. But after a while, the workload was so demanding and the money he was able to make so lucrative, that he ended up creating a business around it.

Calling his computer services GEEK SUPPORT SERVICES (or GEEKSS) for short, he issued invoices for various innocuous tasks such as network maintenance, computerized consulting, and viral protection software (Yes, he had even developed a popular virus protection and firewall program that he distributed a freemium version of, but which had advanced capabilities for a low monthly fee); half of the time, the invoice stated service X, but they really got service Y, which was some sophisticated hack, and the money issued to him was far higher than the minor amount that appeared on the official invoice.

So, in the guise of offering a GEEKSS service, Scotty had come up to Sudbury to meet with a client, but was able to perform the "dutiful son" role as well. He hadn't often been able to combine his personal work-life preferences with a family duty, and so relished the opportunity.

But, as the morning dragged on, and the hospital staff kept popping in to advise them that the surgeon who was scheduled to see Scotty's father had been delayed, yet again, with complications in the earlier scheduled surgery, Scotty became anxious.

He father, ever the jester, had joked about the delay.

"Maybe," he said, leaning over to where Scotty had his nose buried in *Cuckoo's Egg* by Clifford Stoll, and indicated with a sideways jab of his thumb an older gentleman who had been sleeping quite undisturbed for the past hour despite the hub-bub of the waiting area filled with no less than a dozen patients and their families "I'll slip my identification wrist bracelet onto that old fart and slip out of here, pop down to the lake and throw a line into the water. Might as well see if I can pull a trout or two out of the lake while I'm waiting."

Scotty smiled at his father. It had always been about the fishing, hadn't it?

"Go ahead," Scotty had grinned. "I'll create a distraction across the room while you make the switch and slip out."

The two men laughed, but Janelle Desmond, Scotty's mother and Lionel's wife, just shook her head at them before returning her attention to the paperback romance novel she had brought.

Scotty thought about that. Both he and his mother had brought a book to keep themselves occupied while waiting.

Mark Leslie

But not his father.

Nope. Lionel Desmond could easily just sit there, content to be consumed by whatever he reflected on while he sat there stoically observing all of the other people in that hospital waiting room. And he had always been like that for as long as Scotty could remember. It didn't matter where, it didn't matter when, Lionel Desmond would either sit like a statue or seem to take in the surroundings entirely, or he would, on occasion, connect with those around him, often injecting his trademark brand of humor into a situation, putting others around him at ease.

Amazing how he could "work a room" like that – seem to almost instinctively determine what a room needed best – either solitude and quiet reflection, which he seemed to do well (and something that likely lent to his ability to sit for hours in a boat on a lake while fishing, just floating there quietly in the calm tranquility of the natural surroundings, absorbing the world around him and patiently waiting for that tug on his fishing line), or forging relationships with strangers and helping to put others at ease.

It was a skill that neither Scotty nor his mother seemed to possess. And, though he occasionally found himself offering the world a bit of his father's bizarre brand of humor, Scotty didn't seem to possess that natural ability to blend and mix with people, to forge friendships and quickly attained relationships.

He was more analytical, introspective, and good with inanimate objects, data and puzzles. Which was likely one of the reasons he adapted so easily to computer programming. He could easily consume himself with a programming challenge for days without tiring of it. But engaging in the small talk associated with colleagues and friendships was taxing to him.

He would do it out of necessity, of course, but would much rather spend his time focused on code, on exploring the intricacies of the manner by which a string of characters in a particular format could command the control of a computer-controlled environment.

It was likely the reason he didn't have many friends.

No, he could count, on a single hand, the number of people besides his parents that he had forged any lasting relationship with – something that lasted longer than the time associated with a particular chapter of his life.

There were no high school friends that he maintained contact with; except for Pierre, his childhood neighbor, someone he saw and spoke to only when he returned home to visit his parents, and Mr. Prescott, the computer science teacher whom he had maintained regular email contact with since that first day he began to take Scotty under his wing.

Even his relationships through university didn't seem to last longer than the term by which he shared a classroom with someone, or the year he was dorm room-mates with another person.

And the colleagues he had worked with remained just that – colleagues.

So no, there were no long term relationships, no natural inclination, like his father, to bridge those personal connections, to reach out to those around him, to inject a sense of belonging and empathetic understanding into a room.

Even while nervously waiting for his kidney surgery, more than two hours delayed and still not having had a bite to eat nor a single sip of water beyond dinner the evening before, his father sat in the waiting room calmly observing those around him and occasionally offering a friendly nod or quick quip meant to inspire a smile.

Lionel Desmond was indeed a unique character.

Scotty didn't properly "get that" the morning he had spent waiting with his parents in the operating room, dividing his time between trying to read Cuckoo's Egg and thinking anxiously about the meeting he had planned in order to take on what seemed like some intriguing freelance hacking work.

No, it wasn't until much later that Scotty understood there was more to his father than he had ever paid attention to.

It wasn't, perhaps, until the day Scotty had seen his father, eighteen months after he had supposedly died on an operating recovery room table, that he figured there was much more to the man than anybody in his life had ever properly suspected.

But that morning, Scotty was frustrated and anxious, and eager to do nothing more than see his father get into the operating room so that he could get to his meeting and explore the possibility of a new hacking assignment, a new computer challenge.

Chapter Three

Today

Scott stood and watched as the guard slowly walked toward him, his right hand coming up with a Taser.

Then he turned to look over his shoulder and saw Herb walking toward him from the other side, his gun drawn.

"You cannot evade us!" the two said in perfectly matching tones.

"Shit, shit, shit!" Scott said, spotting the empty meeting room to his immediate right. He immediately ducked into the room and slammed the door behind him. Then he locked it and dragged one of the three meeting room tables over to it, flipped it over on its side and pushed it up against the door.

Someone slammed against the door from the other side.

Scott knew it wouldn't hold. Besides, the guard likely had a key to the room.

There wasn't a phone in this twelve by eighteen foot meeting room, just a few more tables, a half dozen chairs, a whiteboard and a single window. But even if there had been a phone who could he call? Building security? They were obviously in on it with Herb, whatever it was.

And what the hell was it with the monotone robot-like voice, the matching glazed look on their faces?

There wasn't time to think about that, to try to understand it. They weren't just trying to capture him. Herb had made the intent quite clear. The goal was to kill him.

Scott needed to find a way out by any means possible.

He rushed to the window as someone again slammed against the door.

There were no latches to open the window, just a thick sheet of glass. Scott looked out, knowing that there was a drop down to the 3rd floor roof-top turret below.

Scott set down his backpack. He lifted one of the wheeled archback office chairs, then threw it against the window. The chair bounced off.

"Dammit!" he yelled as someone again slammed against the door from outside.

He picked up the chair again, and once more threw it against the window.

This time a spider-web of cracks splintered out.

Now we're getting somewhere.

The third time he launched the chair against the window, the spider-web cracks shot out farther across the surface of the window.

Scott heard a key being inserted into the door's lock.

He hefted the chair again, this time shattering the glass completely.

Scott grabbed his bag, looped it over his shoulder, and stepped up into the window. The broken edge of the glass sliced into his left hand as he pulled himself into the window's opening.

The door behind him opened and slammed against the table he had tossed in front of it.

"You cannot evade us!" a robotic voice stated.

Scott jumped out the window to the rooftop alleyway one floor below. When his feet hit, he folded his legs beneath him and rolled out of the fall, losing his backpack in the process.

Rolling several times, Scotty moved up into a crouched position about a foot away from the chair he had thrown through the window. He then rushed to the edge of the roof that overlooked the building's parking lot. There was no fire escape stairway or any other means of climbing down or up. And there was no way that he was going to be able to survive a leap down three stories onto the pavement.

He raced back to the chair, picked it up and launched it against one of the third story windows into another vacant meeting room.

This time, the window cracked upon first impact.

Scott picked the chair up again, this time feeling a sharp pain in his left hand. A line of blood leaked down from his palm and over his wrist. He threw the chair again. The crack became bigger.

He glanced back up at the window he had just jumped out of. Neither Herb nor the security guard was visible. They were obviously still trying to get into the room.

He picked up the chair again. Threw it. The window spider-webbed into a road map havoc of cracks.

Another throw. Deeper and more intense cracks.

"Come on!" Scott yelled, hefting the chair again with all of his might.

The fourth throw did the trick and the glass imploded inward along with the chair.

Scott picked up his backpack, threw it over his shoulder and ducked into the window just as he heard, again in unison, the two men say in that eerie robotic tone. "You won't get away! You cannot evade us!"

Chapter Four

Thirty-Five Years Earlier

"You certainly haven't been fishing," Janelle Desmond's voice cut through the quiet morning, waking Scotty from a deep, restful sleep. "So where in the hell have you been?"

Scotty's eyes snapped open and he flipped over onto his back, rubbing his eyes. The sheets and blanket were warm and snug and cocoon-like around him. His parents rarely ever fought or argued, so hearing his mother's voice in such a loud pitch was particularly startling. The child looked over at the square bright red numerals on the bedside clock radio. It was 9:43 AM. Sunday morning.

Scotty's father had left Friday after work on a solo fishing trip up north. He usually returned from his weekend fishing ventures early on Sunday. And he was usually home just about an hour after the sun got up. He would normally stick his head into Scotty's room and say something like: "Up and at 'em, Chip!" (his fond fatherly nickname for Scotty) and "Time to take on the day" or "The day isn't getting any younger!"

But this morning, he must have arrived a bit later, and there was none of the regular "annoying" fatherly intrusion into his pre-teen desire to sleep most of the morning away. Sundays had always been for sleeping in because Saturday was all about getting up early – yes, even earlier than during the school week – in order to absorb the plethora of cartoons that played.

Scotty often relished in getting up before the channel even came live.

On Saturdays he would wake without benefit of any alarm, toss the sheets aside and race to the living room in order to turn the television on, to see the rainbow strips of the test pattern surrounded by a frame of black and with the quiet, persistent single note pitch whining in the background.

He would sit there, transfixed by the screen, proud of the fact that here he was, pre-station go live time, waiting for the magical "world" of Saturday morning television to begin.

The ritual of being there, each Saturday morning to see the test-pattern revert from the static sound and colored screen to the slide-show of Canadian landscapes and cityscapes accompanied by the *National Anthem* was a special moment in Scotty's weekend.

It was like he was there for the dawn of time, the beginning of everything, and he felt a special part of the universe to go from the "nothing-ness" of the overnight test pattern screen to the beginning of the day.

It wasn't until a decade or so later that he would wonder if that was part of the special feeling his father embraced when he sat out on a lake while fishing and watched the Sunday sun come up over the trees.

But that was Scotty's Saturday morning – it was all about being awake to see the day's world begin, through the *National Anthem* and then the stream of cartoons; from *The Flintstones* and *The Bugs Bunny and Road Runner Looney Tunes, Captain Kangaroo, Scooby-Doo,* enjoying having the morning to himself before his mother stirred.

Saturday was a special ritual where, for a certain time, he was the only person in the universe, just waiting for everything to turn on and begin. It was – and this was something he wouldn't consider for at least a decade, not until he was fully entrenched in computer programming – his weekly "reboot."

But Sunday – now *that* was his day to sleep in, to catch up on the rest missed from the morning before. Sunday was usually when he would try to suck as much rest and sleep from the morning as he could before his father woke him – in the same way that, on Saturdays, he would suck as much of the joy of animated television programs that seemed to only play on Saturday morning (with the exception, of course, of *The Flintstones* and *Spider-Man* which did play during the week at noon for half an hour and also just around the time he was having his after school snack).

Except, not this Sunday.

This Sunday was something new. Something he'd never experienced before.

It was strange hearing his mother's high pitched voice cutting through the morning.

Decidedly more disturbing than his father's typical cheesy morning ritual of waking him.

"Fishing!" Lionel Desmond stated in response in a loud, firm, and deep-toned voice, quite remarkably different than the high-toned shriek.

"No, you weren't fishing!" she said.

"Of course I was. Where the hell else would I be?"

"You tell me, Lionel Edward Desmond. You tell me." There was a pause for at least a couple of beats. "Sure, you have your tackle box, you have your rod, you have your overnight bad and you're wearing your fishing gear. But you don't smell like fish..."

"I don't smell like fish because I didn't have any luck! I didn't catch anything."

"Bullshit!" Scotty heard the front door open and then slam shut. "Look at your truck!" She yelled. "It rained most of the weekend. But look at your truck; look at the wheel wells, look at the tires. There's not even the faintest trace of mud anywhere on the truck."

"You're serious?" Lionel replied. "There's no mud?"

"And I said it before, Lionel." There was another pause, as Scotty imagined his mother leaning in, pursuing her lips together and performing a series of sniffs – the same gesture she would often do when trying to determine if Scotty had brushed his teeth. "But you don't smell like fish."

"I told you…"

"No! You don't smell like fish! But you *do* smell like cologne. Why do you smell like cologne, Desmond? Tell me that, huh. Why do you smell like cologne?"

"Seriously?" Lionel said. "There's cologne on my collar because this is the shirt I originally put on Friday after work.

"Tell me, Lionel!"

"Tell you what?"

"Where have you been?"

"Fishing!"

"No, you haven't. You don't smell like fish. Your truck has no mud on it. I want to know where you've been, Lionel!"

"Fishing!" he repeated. A second later the door slammed so hard that there was the sound of glass breaking. Then, half a minute later, the truck door slammed and Lionel heard the truck starting up then pull out of the driveway.

He laid in bed wishing he could just fall asleep and make it go away as he listened to his mother's quiet sobs.

After a minute, the bathroom door closed and locked and his mother's muffled crying seemed louder.

Sighing, Scotty got out of bed and figured he could be useful by going and cleaning up the broken glass.

Mark Leslie

Chapter Five

Today

It was stepping onto the broken glass on the floor as he stepped inside the third floor of the office that sent Scotty's mind back to that morning when he was a child and his parents had been fighting, that his father slammed the door so hard that it broke the small nested door window.

There was something about the distinct crunch of the glass under his shoes that reminded him of the feel and sound of the glass crunching under his slippers as he moved across the kitchen floor in his pajamas to gather up the dustpan from the kitchen counter which was immediately beside the door.

He hadn't thought about that fight in years. But it was the glass that brought his mind there, reminded him of what they had been fighting about.

He hadn't been fishing, Scotty thought. *But had he been having an affair? What if he was doing something else?*

He had to put those thoughts off as he slipped out of the meeting room he had just smashed his way into and made his way down the abandoned and quiet third floor hallway. He had to get out of there before Herb and the security guard made it downstairs.

As he had stepped through the window, he'd heard another shot fire from the fourth floor, and the sound of what Scott figured was the bullet ricocheting off the brick less than a foot from his head. So they were still upstairs at the window, or at least Herb was. But they had to be following him once they saw he had successfully smashed his way inside.

So he didn't have much time.

The only way for them to get down, he knew, was via the front hallway elevator, which was shared between Digi-Life's office and two other building clienteles, and the rustic wooden stairway access, also shared, but a much quicker way to descend a single floor.

Scott raced down the hall and headed past the main stairway access doors, through the kitchen area and over to the metal circular staircase that graced the "front" of the building. Thank goodness for another way up and down, at least between the third, second, and first floors. The fourth floor didn't have that additional access. Except for the make-shift window exit Scott had just devised, there was previously only the two ways down.

The echoes of his footsteps rang loudly on the metal stairs as he quickly descended down and around. He was worried that the sound would carry and they would know where he was, but, given that he was on the third floor and there were only two ways to get out of the building (apart from breaking a window, he supposed), would be heading down at least one more flight. From the third to the second floors there were only two options – the circular metal staircase he was now on or the shared rustic wooden stairs on the opposite side of the front of the building.

There was a fifty-fifty chance of them knowing which way he had taken. Not that they'd have descended so quickly. Not unless they, like he had done, decided to jump down from the fourth to the third floor. Without someone threatening them with a gun, would they really take that risk? Scott couldn't even believe he had done it; not to mention that he hadn't broken something in the act.

As he made it around the final curve of the metal staircase and onto the second floor, Scott could clearly see down to the 1st floor entrance from the open balcony area of the second floor.

All he had to do was move around the balcony, a simple series of three left turns, and make his way down the stairs.

As began to navigate the second corner, out of the corner of his eye he spotted a pair of blue jeans covered legs heading up the stairs from the very bottom. He didn't stop to look to see who it was. So far, the only two people he had bumped into had a crazy glazed look in their eyes, so he wasn't going to take any chances.

He took a quick right turn that would take him to the front stairwell and pressed the blue button that, from the inside, triggered the door to become unlocked for three seconds. From the other side of the door, Scott knew, one needed to tap their passcard against a key reader in order to perform the same task.

Mark Leslie

He slowly opened the door and peeked inside to see if the stairwell was empty. It was. Footsteps echoed. Quickly. No voices. Just what sounded like a pair of feet slapping down quickly. The sounds came from a couple of landings up, but were heading down fast.

Damn.

He wasn't sure getting into this stairwell would be a good idea. Digging his pass card out of his backpack once he got to the first floor could cost him precious few seconds that would have Herb and the guard catch up with him.

He let the door close and looked back down the hallway to the balcony that overlooked the stairs.

The person ascending had made it to the top of the main stairwell, his brown sport-coat covered back to Scott, before turning right to the final small flight to take him all the way up.

Scott turned to his own right and raced down the aisle of the open concept office, past a stream of grouped project team desks, past three separate sitting areas with couches, coffee tables and mini bar fridges, ad hoc team resting and meeting areas for various collaborative tasks.

There was a visible main aisle on the far side that ran adjacent to this one, past two sets of office areas that blocked one side from the other.

Scott ran past the first set of offices and didn't see anyone working at any of the desks.

If there had been anyone there, if they were in on whatever it was that was going on, they would have likely joined in pursuing him – if they weren't they would have

44

likely given him an odd look, wondering why he was racing down the aisle at top speed. Nobody ever did that. It was odd, out of place. Completely unexpected.

Sort of like what had happened to him this morning.

Scott made it to the second set of offices and towards the small doorway that led to the back office kitchen. The server operations guys, the ones most likely to be here working all hours of the day during the course of regular business, had their stations here; the large status screens indicating web traffic, transaction volume and global server status on a series of thirty-seven inch monitors.

One of the server ops guys was here, hunkered down over his desk. It was Gary, the sharp-witted one who had been the first to befriend Scott when he arrived at Digi-Rights; and though Scott didn't really have any friends at this company, there were some good colleagues, and Gary was one of them. During trips into the second floor kitchen, the company's largest kitchen with the most flavors of coffee, the largest selection of fresh fruit and snacks, Scott usually chatted with Gary about the local sports teams if they were both in the kitchen. If not, Scott would pop around the corner just to say "hey" and shoot the shit if Gary wasn't already in the middle of a phone call or a conversation with someone else. Often, when Scott walked past Gary's desk he could see the man toggle between one of the status screens that monitored the servers and an internet sports channel, where he could catch afternoon games and keep up with the various scores.

This corner of the office was, in many ways, Gary's inner sanctum; a comfortable area. It always felt warm and welcoming to Scott, the same way that Gary was warm and welcoming to pretty much anybody that he met. Along with the screens, the two arm chairs and the couch, there were a few posters and a small beer fridge, and always lots of great additional snacks, well beyond the ones the company provided in the kitchen. No, visiting Gary was almost like visiting a buddy's basement bar or man cave. It came with that comfortable, happy feeling.

And not just décor and scenery and treats. Gary had even taken the time, when there weren't many people around, to block off the air vents near his desk. Anybody who was sitting near an air vent consistently complained about just how cold or how hot it could be. In the winter it blew a strong blast of hot air, way too intense for any comfort; and in the summer months, it blasted freezing cold air, decently balanced for anybody who was at least ten feet away, but for those directly underneath it, the temperature was just too cold, and so sweaters and cardigans were worn by those whose desks were under or near the air vents.

But not Gary. In the same way he had hand-selected the furniture and additions to his air, he had taken the time, when none of the "powers that be" were around, and blocked off the direct flow of the air vents. In the sophisticated manner of a good hack (something Scott could really appreciate), Gary had inserted reflow filters inside the vents themselves. Not only was Gary's tampering not visible, but the filters didn't completely block the air flow –

they routed ninety-five percent of the air back and towards the closest three vents several yards away. A direct blockage would have likely caused a "breakdown" or requirement of some maintenance upon which the building's landlord would know Gary had tinkered with the air vents.

Gary had let Scott in on his little secret one time when the two of them, working late one evening and taking a break to watch a Toronto Maple Leafs game go into overtime, Scott commented on how wonderfully comfortable Scott's "hang-out" was – and he couldn't understand how, when Scott's desk was directly below an air vent, that it wasn't terribly uncomfortable like everyone else's adjacent-to-vent location.

"I've got to ensure my guests are comfortable," Gary had said, and then explained to Scott the details of how he had "hacked" the ventilation system to get it to deliver just enough of the heat or cold without the blatant overkill that had been so problematic.

So Gary, always looking out for everyone else, always offering a warm smile and sense of ease, was a good guy, and someone Scott felt he could trust.

Of course, Herb had been a decent boss too, at least until he pulled out a gun and took a shot at Scott's head.

Would Gary also turn homicidal like Herb and the security guard? Scott wondered. He couldn't take that chance.

"Need your coffee that bad, Scotty?" Gary called out as Scott raced past him and into the kitchen.

He didn't respond to Gary as he darted into the kitchen and made a sharp left.

But he did pause for a moment to look back at Gary who was sitting at his desk in front of three screens feeding him some sort of data about the overall health of the company's websites and back end systems – and, likely, a screen that was toggling back over to the monitoring of the basketball, football, baseball, and hockey scores.

Gary was looking him in the eye and had a partially-confused, partially-bemused look.

There was no glassy-eyed stare. He was simply the Gary that Scott knew and liked. Good old Gary.

And somewhere in the building, likely heading this way, were Herb and the security guard, who were trying to kill Scott. Would they also try to kill others? Was Gary in danger if Scott just ran past and didn't warn him?

"What's up, my man?" Gary asked. "You see the game last night?"

Scott stood there, just looking at Gary, wondering if he would "turn" at any minute.

"You okay?" Gary stood up from his chair and walked towards him. "You're acting very weird."

Deciding Gary could be trusted and needed to be warned, Scott remained in the kitchen but just around the corner, and only visible to Gary, gesturing for his friend to step into the kitchen.

"Oh, shit, Gary," Scott said, putting his hands on the man's shoulders. Gary's eyes, previously bemused and concerned, began to fill with fear. Scott kept a close eye on Gary's eyes and facial features, still speculating that

he could "turn" into the glazed madness he had seen earlier. But so far, everything seemed normal with his friend.
"Something bad is going down here."

"It's not the burritos we had yesterday for lunch, is it?"
Gary said, with a very serious look on his face. Scott
loved the manner by which his friend could deliver silly
jokes like that in such a straight fashion. Half of the people
present when Gary pulled this never even picked up on
the subtle humor the man was throwing into the room; but
Scott always did, and felt that much more fond about him
because of it.

Scott laughed.

"No," he took his hands off of Gary's shoulders. "Not
the burritos. Something bizarre and freaky."

"What?"

Scott looked back to the other side of the kitchen, at
the door to the First Aid room, the one with the couch and
the first aid kit, the sink, the refrigerator filled not with
drinks or treats, but with ice packs and other pharmacy-
like items.

"C'mon, let's pop into the First Aid room. There are
some people on their way, and they'll try to kill us. We
need to hide so I can explain."

Mark Leslie

Chapter Six

"Ouch!" the pin prick woke Scott out of an otherwise contented and restful sleep. He had been having a dream that brought him back to the amazing Halloween party he had attended a couple of weeks earlier, the one he had hesitated to go to because there had been mid-terms to study for and, despite being in need of a break, he didn't really have any friends.

But his room-mates had dragged him along to the university student theatre company's house party.

Everybody had dressed up, including his room-mates. One dressed as a pirate, an elaborate one from Pirates of the Caribbean, and the other one had created a costume of one of the characters from *Pokémon*.

Scott, not having planned anything, threw together a last minute costume. Wearing a red sweater and a pair of red track pants, he took a black felt marker and wrote the word "WELL" across the front of his chest.

When people couldn't figure out what Scott was dressed as, he grinned and said "I'm well red." The moans over the bad pun usually earned him a back slap, a fist bump, or a beer raised in toast.

It had been one of the first times he had felt like he actually fit in.

So, half a dozen beers in to the party, he let his normal guard down and found that he had actually enjoyed himself. When he spied, from across the crowded living room, one of his room-mates friends, an eccentric hipster named Wilson, dancing in a very stylized and artistic series of movements, completely oblivious to everyone else, moving his body in a rhythmic almost hypnotized manner, he thought it was one of the funniest things he had ever seen.

Several people had pointed out Wilson's movements, including hip thrusts and rubbing his hands down the side of his own body, a very sensual series of moves, almost the type of thing you'd see a strip dancer performing, and which seemed to make people either uncomfortable or inspire laughter.

Despite the reaction of the people around him, Wilson danced on, completely oblivious to the attention, to the laughter, and all that.

Scott did something completely out of character, particularly given that he usually just quietly sat back when in a crowd and barely even contributed to the group conversation. He moved in behind Wilson and started dancing with him in the same sensual and rhythmic fashion, spooking the hip thrusts, the ritualized masturbatory-style movements, making the crowd laugh even louder.

"Go Scotty!" someone called. "Yay, Wilson!"

The other dancers parted ways and made room for Wilson and Scott to perform their dance, Wilson still oblivious and Scott enjoyed this unique experience of being at the center of attention.

People cheered and applauded, laughing as Scott continued to partially mock Wilson's moves, but adding his own unique flair and character.

"Well read!" someone cheers. "Well danced!"

Within a minute, another person, one of the hot redheads Scott had his eye on most of the evening who was dressed in a revealing sexy Pocahontas costume, had joined in, mimicking Wilson's thrusts and rubs; then another, and another. She danced really close to Scott, rubbing her thighs and legs against his, running her hands along his sides. Scott swayed into her and their bodies rubbed together in a sexually stimulating way.

The crowd cheered, and within seconds another female joined in, then another guy, another woman, another guy. Soon the entire living room had been writhing together; everybody bumping and grinding and caressing each other in an orgy-like dance festival.

The redhead stayed close to Scott the whole time, and, even though both of them rubbed and caressed the other people around them, moving with the throbbing and pulsing sexualized crowd, they favored each other quite deliciously.

She made and held eye contact with him for extended periods, particularly when she grinded her pelvis against his throbbing erection. Through a subtle twinkling in her gorgeous green eyes she was letting him know that she could feel his growing excitement and relished it.

Scott, still a virgin, had never done or been part of any sort of kissing or petting session with anyone; having this hot redhead lavish such incredible attention on him completely blew his mind. He kept losing himself in her jade eyes, completely overwhelmed with just how beautiful she was. An hour earlier, when he had been admiring her across the room, as she'd been talking to her friends and twirling a finger through the curls of red-brown locks, he wondered what it might be like to touch her hair, to lean in and smell it.

So he did just that. He leaned forward, nestled his nose into the curls of her hair and breathed in. The scent, a citrus-herbal combination, filled his being. "You're the most beautiful thing I have ever seen, touched, or smelled," Scott whispered in her ear as he gently nipped and licked the lobe.

She squirmed beneath him as he did that and rubbed even harder.

All around them, other couples were doing the same sort of thing. But not just couples; there were groups of three and four people all grinding together, running hands all over one another, swaying in rhythm, hands, groins, buttocks rubbing, bumping and grinding. Several were kissing; and not just the intimate kissing of the same couple, but lips and mouths exploring multiple different pairs of others, briefly pecking some while lingering more sensually on some others. Some people moved from group to group, participating in a very "social butterfly" type of activity, working the room, making the rounds.

Occasionally, a third and fourth person would join in on the action with Scott and the gorgeous redhead, fondle them both, rub up against one another. But the way the two of them moved so closely in unison, those who joined quickly moved on to another group, recognizing that there was something a bit more intense going on here and getting the hint.

At one point, he reached out, caressed both sides of her face with his hands, and then let them slowly trail down to tickle her throat then slide down to her breasts. She pushed her breasts up against the palms of his hands and he gently rubbed them, feeling her rock-hard nipples poking through, responding eagerly to his caress.

She placed her own hands on the sides of his face and pulled his face in, her hot wet tongue thrusting into his mouth; her hands then moved down, all while they still writhed and danced and pushed up against each other, trailed down his back and clenched at his buttocks and pulled him in tighter to her, pushing and rubbing her pelvis against his aching hard penis.

At one point Scott slipped two fingers of his right hand under the fabric covering her breast and swirled one around the stiff nipple – she leaned in closer to him, something Scott didn't think was possible and let out a beautifully seductive moan in his ear, saying, "I've never wanted anybody so much."

They danced like that, making virtual love right in front of everybody else on the dance floor, their tongues mixing, their hands eagerly exploring one another's contours. As Scott rubbed her nipple with his right hand, his other hand on her ass and pulling her up against him, he felt her shudder and shake and let out a deep sigh.

When she finished shuddering against him, an incredible experience that lasted almost a full minute, she whispered in his ear again. "I just had one of the most incredible extended orgasms."

Scott completely lost it at that point, felt himself erupt and come all over himself, completely soaking his underwear and track pants.

She pushed against him harder, realizing that he was coming and, pulling him tight against her, whispered again in his ear. "Thank you, Scott. That was absolutely incredible. Sex has never been like that before. I never realized just how incredible it could be."

The let-down feeling brought Scott back to his normal state. He didn't even realize that she knew his name. He just felt extremely uncomfortable with ejaculating all over himself, worried about the growing wet spot on his crotch.

"Thank you," he whispered. "You are the most beautiful woman I have ever seen. I love you." And then he turned and made his way off of the dance floor, left the party and half-ran, half-walked back to the apartment.

A classic Scott move.

He had been dreaming about the beautiful redhead, about the incredibly intense feeling, about how amazing it had been; all ruined because of his social awkwardness. In the dream, he was confident and strong, not shy and nervous and weak. And in the dream, he certainly hadn't followed up the evening with the stupidity of coming on too strong. In the dream, none of that was present. It was pure emotion, pure pleasure, just like that night had been.

That's when, in the midst of the dream, he had felt this sudden sharp pricking pain and it woke him right out of the wonderful memories of the gorgeous redhead whose name he never even learned.

He sat up from the sleeping bag, rubbing his shoulder where he'd felt the prick.

It was dark and there was the odd odor of propane gas and mustiness in the air that quickly overtook Scott's fond memories of the special scent of that sexy woman's hair.

Scott remembered that he had been on an overnight fishing trip with his father; that, on this early November weekend, they had been somewhere far up Highway 144 in mid-northern Ontario, at a special fishing spot his father had picked out. And, despite the cold, there they were, hunkered in the middle of nowhere and partaking in a father/son venture in a trailer.

"Dad! What the hell?"

"Sorry, son." Lionel Desmond said, and Scott could see, from the light of a gas lantern on the far side of the trailer, the pop-out spot where his father had been sleeping, his father fiddling with the bottom compartment of his tackle box, hastily putting something away. "I must have poked you with the stem of my poppy when I was looking for the little yellow flashlight on your bunk."

His father indicated the little red molded plastic with green flacking that was fastened to the plaid fishing shirt with a pin. His father had always been a stickler for wearing the poppy, part of a Canadian and UK tradition of commemorating the servicemen and servicewoman who have been killed in conflicts since 1914. In Canada, Remembrance Day was celebrated each November 11th (part of the 11th hour of the 11th day of the 11th month, a date significant because it that time in 1918 when the First World War officially ended) and from the beginning of November, Canadians wore the red poppies over their hearts as a symbol that they remembered.

Before the general public started wearing them, news anchors and other public officials were usually the first the begin sporting the red plastic flowers on their collars.

Lionel Desmond, so long as Scott could remember, always took Remembrance Day very seriously. He would start wearing the poppy at least one full week before Halloween, even when it was common for most of the rest of society to begin wearing it on November 1st. And he had always booked November 11th off work, always attended the parade and ceremony that took place downtown at the Cenotaph.

Scott remembered the time when he was little and, at the ceremony in the blistering cold and snow, during the two minutes of silence, time meant to be spent in quiet reflection, Scott and his school chum, Edward Leroux had been making silly faces at one another. Two minutes to a seven year old could seem like an excruciatingly long amount of time. Standing across from him, Edward was crossing his eyes and sticking out his tongue. Scott smiled and then found himself hitching as he tried to control giggling out loud.

The only sound was the wind, the occasional sniffle or cough from one of the three hundred people standing in silence in such a tight area; and, very quietly, Scott's heavy breathing as he tried to hold the laughter in.

His father had caught his eye and sent him such a dire and stern warning that the giggles immediately vanished. And, afterwards, Lionel Desmond not only threw his son over his knee with his pants pulled down and proceeded to spank him with the thick leather strap that was used in the Desmond household for corporal punishment – a spanking that lasted a full two minutes and left Scott with a burning and throbbing backside that he couldn't comfortably sit down on for the rest of the day, but there was a lecture and a learning experience to be had.

Yes, there had always been a learning experience to be had with Lionel Desmond.

The day after the painful spanking, Lionel sat his son down and told him, again, the story of Lionel's father, Scott's grandfather and how the man had given his life for their country as a soldier in World War II. How Lionel, who was only two years old when his father died overseas, didn't even have more than a single fleeting memory of his Dad.

"Tens of thousands of men and women gave their lives, sacrificed themselves, and went to serve the common good, in order for us to have the freedoms that we now have." Lionel explained. "And despite them giving up so much, putting themselves directly in the path of harm's way, virtually the only thing that we do is once a year, we wear a poppy on our chest, we attend a ceremony to honor them and we give two minutes of silence in respect for all that they have done.

"Two simple minutes. That's all that is asked. Two minutes of reflection, of quiet, of respect." His face turned red as he spoke. "Is that pittance of time really too much to ask for?"

After the lecture, Lionel made Scott write out "In Flanders Fields" the classic poem written by the Canadian solder, Lieutenant Colonel John McCrae after presiding over the funeral of a friend and fellow soldier, two dozen times. Then, he forced his son to read *Generals Die in Bed* a classic world war one book by Charles Yale Harrison, *The Wars* by Timothy Findley, *Night* by Elie Wisel, and *D-Day* by Stephen E. Ambrose.

Scott liked reading, but was overwhelmed with the message that was spoken through the books. He didn't complain, and worked his way through them over the course of the rest of the month. The books moved him, terrified him, inspired him, and made him think. Upon completing them he was actually interested in reading more and understanding more, and so picked up *The Diary of Anne Frank* and *The Rise and Fall of the Third Reich* by William L. Shirer.

At the end of that November, when his father knew he had read the four books, he never spoke with his son about it again, never talked about the books or asked Scott to share his thoughts upon reading them.

All that he did was sit down across from his son at the breakfast table one morning, and said: "Do you see, now, what I mean? Do you understand now, just a little bit of what it was like? Do you get why I take Remembrance Day so seriously?"

At that point, he pulled his wallet out of his back pocket, opened up a compartment and took out a small square white and brown picture of a young soldier who couldn't be more than eighteen or nineteen. A peaked solder cap on his head, and a lopsided grin suggested the world was his oyster and there was a whole universe ahead of him that he eagerly embraced.

Scott had never seen the picture before but he knew, without his father saying another word, that this was his grandfather, his dad's father.

"I might only wear a poppy for a couple of weeks in October and November each year, but I carry this picture around with me all of the time. I wear my father's memory every single day."

All Scott could do was nod, with a single tear running down his face.

He had got it.

And from that day on, Scott himself took Remembrance Day very seriously.

Nowhere as seriously, though, as his father.

Scott could remember, in fact, that no matter where he was or what he was doing, Lionel Desmond would wear the poppy for the whole period between October 24th and November 11th. Even out here, in the middle of nowhere, where nobody would see him, he still wore the red flower on his shirt. When Scott asked him why he wore it even when nobody could see, his father turned to him, a very serious look on his face, and said: "I'll see it. I'll know. It's not just for show. It's just as much for me."

There was one year that Scott never forgot, shortly after his father's gall bladder surgery, when, upon returning home but still not recovered enough to go back to work, spending most of the day in bed in his pajamas, Scott witnessed the man, who could barely stand because he was in so much pain, get up and stand quietly during the two minutes of reflection on the 11th hour of the 11th day of the 11th month.

Lionel Desmond took remembering very seriously, and there was no thing or nobody who could ever or would ever take that away from him.

He would always remember.

Scott always thought the poppy's design, with the single stick pin, might have purposely been fashioned in the way that it was because, each year he suffered no less than a dozen prickings, a side effect of the simplistic design. Perhaps that was a good thing, since the poppy was there to remind us of the way in which soldiers suffered and gave their lives for our freedom. A little pin prick every once in a while was a sharp and simple reminder that our minor woes are nothing in comparison.

Having been pricked by poppies hundreds of times over the years, Scott rubbed at his shoulder, confused. His shoulder hurt far more than any poppy stabbing he'd ever experienced before.

"What were you doing leaning so close to me?" Scott asked, still rubbing his shoulder, considering taking the long sleeve shirt he had been sleeping in to see if he was bleeding. But the subtle puffs of his breath in the air reminded him of the intense cold, a cold that was already starting to seep in now that he had been sitting up and out of the cocoon of his sleeping bad.

Strange, he thought, *that the poppy could poke through not only my shirt, but also my sleeping bag.*

"The flashlight was stuck between the mattress and the canvas wall," his father said. "I had to lean in really far to get ahold of it. Looks like I really stabbed you good."

"You did that all right," Scott said.

"Sorry." Lionel closed the tackle box and shoved it under the bench desk he was sitting at, in the small kitchen area of the pop-up trailer. "Well since you're up, we should get out on the lake. It's almost five-thirty."

Mark Leslie

Chapter Seven

Today

After hustling quickly into the nurse's room on the second floor of Digi-Life's Liberty Village office, Scott slowly closed the door behind them, careful to ensure the latch didn't click too loudly. Then he carefully engaged the lock before turning back to Gary.

His friend had a concerned look on his face.

"You're freaking me out, Scotty," Gary said. "What's going on here?"

"I wish I knew," Scott said. "I'm really not sure what is going on or why it is happening, but Herb is trying to kill me."

"Herb Canter?"

"Yeah."

Gary's face took on an odd expression, a look Scott recognized immediately – it was the one people normally reserved for when a crazy person cornered them on the street or in a shopping mall. It was a combination of a subtle "deer in the headlights" lift to the eyes combined with the quick eye-darting that suggested the person, feeling backed into a corner, was looking for any opportunity to escape the situation. There was no fight or flight about this; it was all pure flight, because they prey understood that there was no rational way of defeating this foe in the "hand to hand" combat of normal socially acceptable conversion. No, the crazy person was following a specific agenda, performing a script that nobody else had access to, and would take you down the pre-determined path they controlled entirely. Usually, the crazy person, completely oblivious to normal social convention, would never pick up on the subtle nature of the terrified and cornered person's eyes; they would, if they even noticed anything much in the face of the person they were speaking to, in the bull-headed following of their precious script, would likely have interpreted the wide-eyed look to be that of genuine and unabashed interest.

That is what the look on Gary's face told Scott.

"I'm not crazy," he said, doing his best to speak in a calm and rational voice. He knew, having put Gary into that 'Oh no, I'm speaking with a person who has lost their marbles' state, that it would be difficult to navigate without everything sounding a little bit crazy to him.

"I was working at my desk on the fourth floor," Scott said, "when Herb called me in to his office. He at first seemed normal, but there was a strange glazed look on his face, and a very subtle almost robotic tone to his speech.

"I didn't think much about it at first. I mean, it is still early, for all I knew, Herb hadn't had his morning cup of coffee and was still working off one too many the night before.

"But he tells me to close the office door, and the next thing I know he's taking a shot at my head."

"He what?"

"He fired a bullet at my head."

"With a gun?"

"Yeah, a handgun of some sort."

"There's no way. I would have heard it. Those things are loud."

"It must have had some sort of muffler or silencer on it, because it didn't make a loud noise, just a strange sound. Because I had my back turned, I thought the sound was Herb smacking a thick plastic ruler down hard on his desk – you know how as a student you used to hold it down firm with one hand, but with the other hand, slowly pry and bend the ruler back so it would snap down hard against the desk. *That* is exactly what it sounded like.

"So there I am, shocked by the sudden hole punched through the drywall beside me and the dust and smoke, when I hear this sound. I turn and duck at the same time, and see Herb is holding a gun."

"No way,"

"Yeah, and he says, in this strange, robotic voice: *'You won't get away. You cannot evade us.'*"

"Us?"

"Yeah. So I figure Herb has lost it, worked way too many sixteen hour days. I mean, my work is pretty solid, so there's no way it was a performance issue."

Gary issued a nervous laugh into the room.

"But I figure he's whacked. So I duck down and half-crawl half run out of the room, run around the corner, eager to get the hell away from there, when I see this security guard coming down the hall toward me.

"Safe, I figure. I'm safe now.

"But do you know what he says to me when I tell him about Herb?"

"What?"

"He says: '*You won't get away. You cannot evade us.*' In that same robotic tone. As his eyes are just as glazed as Herb's were.

"No!"

"Yeah. I figure, holy crap, I'm in a bad sci-fi thriller now. But I know, immediately, that I'm toast, so I run from the guard. Soon enough both Herb and the guard are after me, repeating that line again and again."

Scott then proceeded to explain the rest of the story to Gary. As he told the tale, he injected bits of humor into it, like he had about the work performance joke when Herb shot at him. Given their jovial relationship and the way they liked to make fun cracks at one another, he knew Gary would realize he wasn't crazy if he told the story, as unbelievable as it was, with a bit of a sense of consistency for their relationship. Gary was an analytical person, he knew – he would believe even a difficult to accept story if all of the elements that, otherwise, made complete sense, lined up.

So, though Scott didn't have all that much skill as a conversationalist, being a hacker, someone used to guiding a program through logical steps; particularly logical steps that, while deviating from the original outline and intent of the program, still seemed normal and not at all out of place, was just part for the course.

"Do you think it's just the two of them?" Gary asked, when he got to the point of bumping in to his friend on the second floor. "Or could there be more. I mean," he pulled out his mobile phone and they both glanced down at it, "should we call 9-1-1?"

A sound outside the door, the scuffle of footsteps, startled them both.

Mark Leslie

Chapter Eight

Thirty Years Earlier

"A lock, Dad?" Scotty had said, with the perfectly blended inflection of despise mixed with the emboldened question of authority that one expects from virtually any fourteen year old.

"Fishing lures are expensive," his father replied without turning his back.

Lionel Desmond had been sitting at his workbench and puttering with one of the gigs with a pair of needle-nose pliers and a stretch of fishing line when his son, moping around from room to room, bored during the March break, stood behind his father and watched him work. Scotty had been there a few minutes, curious to see what his father had been doing, but bored with being bored, and noticed, not for the first time, that the tackle box sitting on the right hand side of his father's workshop bench had a small lock affixed to it.

"People steal fishing lures?" the tone of his voice suggested he was speaking with an idiot. It was a tone that had come natural, and often, from the young man, and not just when speaking to his father, but when speaking to virtually anybody. Not that, unless he was called upon in school, he spoke much.

Mr. Prescott, his computer teacher, might have been the only person Scotty regularly spoke with where he didn't use that tone. Heck, Prescott might have been the only person Scotty would have considered a friend.

"Yes," Lionel said. "They do. People steal fishing lures all the time,"

"Losers," Scotty huffed.

"I have close to eight hundred dollars of lures and other fishing accoutrements in this box."

"Eight hundred?"

"Yes."

"I thought you made a lot of the lures yourself."

"I do. But even the parts can cost a lot of money."

"Really?"

For the first time in months, the tone in Scotty's voice changed, and Lionel Desmond immediately sensed it. The query wasn't layered with contempt and ire; it was a genuine element of interest and intrigue.

Lionel turned from what he was doing and looked his son in the eyes. It had been years since Scotty had taken any sort of interest in anything his father had to say. He sat a bit more straight on the stool in front of his workbench, his shoulders back and his check poking out.

"Yes. Have a look at this one here. I special ordered it through Ramako's in Sudbury. It cost me about one hundred and sixty bucks. I took this painted agile crankbait, combined it with a monster grub I ordered through eBay and added my own layers of reflective tri-color paints. The total cost comes to just over three hundred."

"Wow."

"I know. Who would have thought fishing could be such an expensive hobby."

The temporary lifting of the bile in Scott's voice fled, as he considered something and again challenged his father with another question.

"So people might break into your truck and steal the tackle box. Okay, I get that. But why do you keep it locked when it's in the house? It's not like Mom or I would even care to peek inside."

Lionel Desmond's shoulders sank back down a little as he realized the interest and lack of despise was just a fleeting thing.

"It's just a habit, I suppose," he said.

Mark Leslie

Chapter Nine

Today

The door handle to the first aid room turned. First left, then right. Something, most likely a shoulder, bumped up against the door. But it was locked, and wasn't going to budge.

Scott raised a single finger and placed it vertically against his pursed lips.

Gary shook his head, the look on his face saying, *Are you nuts? Do you think I'd be stupid enough to make any sort of noise?*

The door handle turned, one more time.

The vent immediately above the door suddenly came on, sending down a stifling blast of head right onto Scott's forehead, the noise and warmth startling him so much that he almost let out an audible yelp.

As he watched the doorknob turn, he flashed back to one of many scenes from *The Walking Dead*, an AMC television program that he had gotten hooked on a few years back. Set in a post-apocalyptic world that has been over-run with some sort of zombie virus, a few remaining survivors do their best to stay alive, trying to stay one step ahead of the mindless flesh-eating resurrected dead, known by the main characters as "walkers" but also trying not to get killed by the other survivors.

It was in one of the very first episodes that the main character, Rick, who had been in a coma while the world had been going to hell, was taken in by a pair of strangers, a father and son team. In the night, the time when the zombies were most active, they had stood near the front door to their house, panicked looks in their eyes as a zombie on the other side of the door tried their door.

As Scott watched the knob turn, he couldn't help but flash back to that episode. Although, admittedly, thought there were no zombies outside the door, there was something much worse. One of the two men who had been trying to kill him.

That was far worse than any imagined creature on a network television program.

Sweat leaked down Scott's brow and into his eyes. He couldn't be bothered to try to wipe it away.

Damn heating in this building, Scott thought, realizing that being closed in with another person and having the heat pumped in like that was extremely uncomfortable. Of course, the fact Scott had been running didn't help matters; not to mention the danger he had been running from.

No, not *running*.

Evading.

The words of both Herb and the security guard echoed in his head. *You cannot evade us*.

The knob stopped turning and the footsteps shuffled away.

Scott reached up, wiped the sweat from his eyes, and looked back at Gary, who was quietly staring back. He hadn't bothered to wipe the sweat from his own eyes.

The footsteps moved to the second door down this short hallway, to the supply closet, a room the same size as the first aid room; a six by twelve foot room, this one filled with various office supplies – paper, pens, folders, whiteboard markers, and other office paraphernalia. Scott knew the office was kept locked before nine and after five in order to maintain tighter control on what Digi-Life termed "unnecessary shrink" – employees taking additional office supplies for use, not in the office, but in their homes, as part of their children's school supplies or for other non-work related needs.

Scott and Gary remained quiet as they listened, imagining the person was trying the supply room door; it too being locked.

Then the footsteps shuffled off back towards the kitchen area.

Seconds later, a second pair of footsteps could be heard approaching to join the first pair. No voices, just the footsteps moving in unison.

Eerie, Scott bemused. *How very much like zombies.* He shook his head.

He had imagined that Herb and the security guard, if that's who these two were outside the door, had split up and each taken a different path on the second floor. With one of them taking the hallway to the left, and the other to the right, they would end up coming at Scott either of the two ways he might have run.

He figured that they likely had checked every single room on the second floor, including the bathrooms. There were at least eight offices and meeting rooms, mostly on the far side of this floor. The kitchen, the first aid room, and the supply closet beside the first aid room would be the last three places to check.

The question is, why weren't they communicating with one another, and, more importantly, what would they do, where would they go now?

Without speaking a word, the footsteps could be heard heading back down the hall by the first aid room and supply closet. One pair then clomped down the stairs on the other side of the hallway, while the others, obviously not on the stairs, must have headed back to the front of the second floor in order for them to sweep the first floor, its offices and meeting rooms, and likely rendezvous somewhere in the middle.

Waiting until the footsteps had receded far enough away that he couldn't hear them any longer, Scott let out a sigh of relief and then turned to Gary.

"Okay," he whispered. "They're gone. We have to figure out the best way to get past them and out of here."

Gary didn't respond.

He stood there, quietly blinking.

"Gary?"

A vacant, glassy-eyed look started to slowly come over his friend's face and his eyes temporarily rolled back in their sockets.

"Gary?" Scott said again, waving a hand in the air between them. "Gary, speak to me."

After a couple of seconds, Gary's eyes rolled back to normal. He blinked, shook his head a bit. Blinked again. Then he looked directly at Scott again, as if waking up from some sort of foggy state. But the glazed look – that same glazed look he had seen in Herb and the security guard became evident on Gary's face.

"You won't get away. You cannot evade us," Gary uttered in a monotone robotic voice.

Mark Leslie

Chapter Ten

Seventeen Years Earlier

Scott found a few more pictures of his grandfather in his father's tackle box. That and a few other objects he couldn't quite understand.

He might have gone fishing with his father, and grew up in a home where fishing was important, so Scott didn't know what every single lure, reel attachment or gadget for fishing was. But he had seen a few of those objects quite by accident one afternoon when he'd been looking for a simple pin.

Scott was home for a visit with his parents; he had recently graduated from university and had been working part-time at a local Radio Shack as a sales clerk while taking on simple computer repair, home networking setup and illegal satellite and digital receiver card hack jobs on the side. Due to the part-time nature of his weekly commitments (which saw him working less than twenty-four hours each week) and the fact he could set his own hours for the side-jobs, Scott could easily craft four day weekends, making the trek from Toronto to his parent's home simple enough.

Being the only son of Lionel and Jeanette Desmond, Scott was regularly guilt-tripped into making the trek back home, and he did so at least once a month. It wasn't much of a hardship actually, but still, the fact that he had always felt obligated to do so was like a ball and chain that slowed him down, held him from being able to really branch out.

Not that he'd had any real ambitions.

He was content to do the computer mucking and hacking that he liked so well and spend the majority of his free time playing video games.

And, since most of the games he was currently into could be played on his laptop, it didn't matter whether he was in his own apartment or in his parent's basement for the weekend.

And that's what had happened. He'd been playing a hacked version of *Battle Warworld*, an online immersive 3D first person adventure game; but somewhere in the middle of the adventure he was on, the sysops updated the game – they did that often, pushing down updates into the legitimate system paths that the hacks didn't always pick up on – preventing him from moving further.

Scott had to pause the game and figure out a way to bypass the latest security install.

And that's when he realized he needed a stick-pin, a long sharp and pointy object, in order to pop open the side of the drive case so that he could fiddle with the modified RAM sticks he had been using.

And, though he did have plenty of tools with him – he rarely traveled without the basic core requirements for most of the jobs he performed – he didn't have all the necessary ones to perform the task he'd been hoping for.

And that led him to his father's workshop, and his tackle box. And something a bit more confusing.

The first shock came when he got to the tackle box and saw that the lock his father normally kept on it was detached. The lock had been something that had confused Scott for a long time, despite his father's explanation that it was always on, even when he was at home, out of habit.

He had never seen the tackle box left unlocked – heck, it was rare that his father was ever not at home without his tackle box – so he did what any curious young man would do.

He opened it up, slowly methodically, and a bit worried that there might be an alarm that was set off when the box was opened.

It felt odd, doing this, and Scott had to look back over his should as he was doing it, almost as if he were fourteen and had found his father's secret stash of Playboys and was filled with an excitement mixed with an intense fear of getting caught. He laughed at himself for having that reaction, but still, it had been a completely unexpected thing.

He stared down at the box. Sure, he had seen it opened before, many time. But never when he wasn't in the presence of his father.

He looked down at the tri-sectioned part of the box that folded up and back when the lid opened. It contained about three dozen little inch-wide by inch-long compartments filled with bits of metal, feathers, twigs, ribbons, and other assorted objects. It reminded him a little of his mother's jewelry box, filled with earrings of all shapes, makes, and sizes.

He rubbed his chin, realizing, immediately, that it was the same gesture Indiana Jones had used in The Temple of the Lost Arc in that classic scene where he was about to lift the idol off of the temple, before carefully reaching out and lifting off the top compartment.

On top were a couple of topographic and hydrographic fishing maps folded and layered onto the top of the main compartment.

Scott carefully lifted them out and placed them beside the tackle box.

Beneath those maps were two additional compartments with a click-down lid.

He opened the one on the right and saw that it contained a bunch of larger items, pieces of reels, rods as well as a whistle, a mini flashlight, a bottle of bug-spray, a smelly oil-stained rag, some pencils, a pen, a carpet knife, and a half-used pack of throat lozenges.

The right side contained more of the same type of items – a mishmash of fishing and toolbox materials.

Scott frowned, wondering what was bothering him about this set up.

When he leaned back he realized what it was. Despite the space required for the top compartment and the additional pair of larger compartments underneath, there was still at least two and an half inches unaccounted for in the bottom of the tackle box.

Carefully removing all of the miscellaneous objects from both of the compartments, he quietly closed the box and lifted it up to look at the bottom and see if, perhaps, the design left some hollow spaces underneath it. Being empty, the partially plastic and partially metal box should have weighed no more than a couple of pounds. But, instead, it weighed perhaps five or even ten pounds.

He placed it back down and picked it up again.

Yeah. Almost ten pounds.

He tilted it first to the left, then to the right. Something heavy slid around inside, metal clinked on metal.

"There is something else in there," Scott said, even more curious now.

He placed the tackle box back down on the workshop bench, again opened it and pried open the lids of the two interior compartments. He slid his fingers around the sides, looking for a gap, a line, anything that might indicate how those compartments opened or lifted out.

Solving this wasn't all that different than looking at the code in a program and understanding how it operated. Through a simple trial and error series of logical steps, Scott fiddled and played with the compartment.

After a few minutes, still not having any success, he heard footsteps upstairs.

"Oh, oh."

He rushed over to the door to the workshop and stuck his head around the corner. His father had been at work and his mother was home. Could his father have returned early?

He heard the sounds of a door opening, the clattering of cups. More footsteps and the sound of coffee being poured.

It was his mother getting a coffee from the kitchen. He followed the sounds of her footsteps back into the living room where she was most likely sipping at her coffee and enjoying a paperback romance novel.

He should have known it wasn't his father from the sound of footsteps. His father had always walked with a distinct and unique lurch-step, the side effect of a motorcycle accident he'd had when he was a young man. Of course, with his nerves running on edge, he forgave himself for being a bit overly sensitive and paranoid.

He let out a deep breath he hadn't realized he had been holding, realizing just how anxious he was.

This was, indeed, more than finding his father's stash of porn magazines. This was a deeper secret, part of the cards Lionel Desmond held close to his chest.

Yes, fishing had always been a significant priority for the man – but this was something more, something that went a lot deeper than the desire to pursue, in Moby Dick fashion, the big one, the one that got away, the elusive perfect catch.

Scott returned to the "empty" tackle box and resumed his exploratory investigation, determined he would get into the secret lower compartment.

Running a list of the various ways he had already poked and prodded, he made a mental tick mark into the concepts and ideas he had already run through so that he wouldn't duplicate his efforts and waste time.

This was, despite the nervousness, despite the fear of being caught, an intriguing and satisfying challenge.

He fiddled for another five minutes, continuing to tick off each new idea of things to try, before he finally figured it out.

It was a trick bottom that operated on a similar principal to the Chinese finger trap puzzle. Placing just the right amount of pressure using opposing forces on the top diametrical corners of the box, he heard a distinct click. And that's when the compartment snapped open and he was able to lift the false bottom out.

This is not a standard tackle box that you can buy at a place like Ramako's Scott thought, as he lifted it out and glanced at the curious objects hidden beneath.

On top of the compartment were some additional maps; ones that seemed to be topographical and hydrographical like the other ones. But they were printed in a different fashion and on a thicker type of paper that the others. He placed them aside and there he spied a series of old brown photographs.

Pictures of his grandfather. He recognized the man's distinctive well-packed eyes. At least, that's how his father had described his dad, when he spoke about him. It was one of the main features he could remember from his father, and in the few pictures Scott had seen, the man's eyes, slightly droopy in nature, seemed to always have large wrinkly sacks under them, as if the man were perpetually overtired.

"My old man's eyes looked like they were always packed and ready to go," Scott's father had said on those occasions where Desmond senior had come up in conversation or reminiscences.

Scott had only ever seen perhaps half a dozen pictures of his grandfather in the various photo albums on the bookshelf in the family room – but here, tucked away and hidden in this secret location of his father's tackle box, were at least a dozen shots he had never seen. The photos were of the same brown and white quality of the ones he had seen before, and featured Reginald Desmond in various stages of his life.

One featured him as a young man, posing with a couple of buddies, shit-eating grins on their faces, their arms draped over one another's shoulders. All three were crew cut like Scott's grandfather, who was in the middle – his swollen eye bags immediately revealing him as the man to the left of the trio. In Reginald's right hand was a beer bottle that he was lifting and tipping towards the camera as if offering a toast.

Another picture was a solo one of Reginald, dressed in his military gear – unlike the bust portrait Scott was used to seeing, this was a full-on full body shot. Reginald was in full dress uniform, hat, tie, etc.; he looked proud to be wearing the uniform.

The picture under that was Reginald, in a picture that had to be of him ten years earlier – this one was of him in uniform as well, but not a military uniform. A Boy Scout uniform. He wore the rounded small cap atop his head, the elegantly tied kerchief around his neck, the dual shaded brown shirt and pant combination. He looked like a soldier in training in that shot. Scott grinned, remembering some professor from an English class he had taken talking about how the Boy Scouts had indeed been a pretraining ground for young men to begin to learn the discipline of joining the military and serving their country.

Several other pictures featured Reginald at about the same age he looked to be in the Boy Scout photo – somewhere in the realm of ten to twelve years old. In them he was either holding a fishing rod in one hand and a tackle box in the other – a shot likely taken when he had been about to embark on his fishing expedition – or he was posing in a shot obviously taken when returning from the trip, holding a swath of eight fish of various sizes dangling beside him.

One of the pictures featured Reginald as a toddler, dressed in a fancy little sailor suit complete with a Donald Duck cap propped on his head. He was sitting back on a couch, his little legs not even reaching to the edge of the couch, and he was leaning forward, his right arm extended toward the camera and in his right hand, an unlit cigarette held between two fingers, as if he'd been an experienced smoker. He looked about to say something he imagined was quite amusing. And, even though he couldn't be much more than a year and a half old, his identity quite clear by the fact that his eyes, though not as puffy and packed as they became later in life, were still full and pronounced.

"What are you doing with all these hidden photos of Grandfather, Dad?" Scott wasn't sure why his father would have gone to such trouble to keep these pictures hidden and in such a secure spot.

Putting the photos aside, he looked down into what else was inside the tackle box, and started pulling them out one by one.

The first object looked like a hearing aid. It had the little ear, shaped crescent that would fit over the top of a person's ear, then a little rounded nub that you might stick inside your ear. Strange, his father had never had or at least spoken about any hearing problems – why, then, would he have this hearing aid? And why would he keep it in his tackle box.

The second object Scott pulled out of the tackle box was a silver metal box no more than an inch high by two inches wide and long. It had a little extendable aerial that you could pull out of the top, a small screen that seemed to be some sort of digital display as well as a couple of analog meters; one rounded one with a pair of small hands and the other that looked like the partial crescent shape of a voltmeter. Below that were a cluster of nine small buttons that looked like a digital telephone keypad, the top six buttons black and the bottom row of three red. Below that was another small screen. Scott lifted the box up, figuring it was about two pounds – pretty dense – and saw that on the left side of the box there were a couple of audio jack ports – two different sizes – one that appeared to be for 3.5 MM mono plugs and the other for the much larger and thicker 35 MM stereo plug. As he twisted it around, he noticed the on/off switch at the back near the top.

"What the hell is this?" Scott mumbled, putting it back down on the workbench.

He wanted to turn it on and play with it, but there were several other strange devices in the tackle box that he was curious to look at.

The third object looked to be some sort of handgun shaped object, except the pistol part ended in a tiny umbrella-shaped object and the butt had a thin antenna. There was an on/off switch.

There was a gold-banded watch inside as well – there appeared to be nothing unique about that.

The last large object was a pill bottle, a somewhat translucent brown plastic and a white lid – but no label and nothing written on the top. He shook it and could hear the pills rattling around inside. Then he pushed down and twisted the lid, but it didn't come off the way a standard child-proof lid was supposed to be removed. The pill bottle seemed to have, much like the false bottom of the tackle box, some special secret way of opening it. Scott fiddled with it for a minute but was unable to decipher the manner by which he could open it.

Finally, in the bottom was a syringe, a couple of bolts, a pen, a pair of cufflinks, a tie clip, and small pile of lose change, both American and Canadian money; mostly nickels and quarters. Scott picked up one of the dimes and noticed there were a series of silver rings near them. He fiddled with one of the silver rings, eventually figuring out there was a thin ring he could pop off to reveal the coin was hollow inside.

"Holy shit, Dad," Scott said. "What the hell would you need hollow coins for? Passing on information about secret fishing spots?"

That's when he heard the front door upstairs open and close, and his father's voice.

"Shit! Shit! Shit!" Scott said, scrambling to place all of the objects back into the bottom of the tackle box. The coins, the pill box, the pistol-shaped object, the watch, the metal box and the hearing aid. Once they were inside, he carefully put his grandfather's pictures back on top, then set the false bottom object back in.

He could hear his father and mother speaking upstairs.

"Don't come downstairs," Scott said. "Don't come downstairs." He repeated that as he struggled with the false bottom, trying to get it to properly latch back into place. It wasn't working. Nothing he tried seemed to be getting it back into place.

The sound of a drawer squeaking open and the clinking of cutlery filled the kitchen, familiar sounds of Scott's mother preparing a meal.

"I'll heading downstairs for a minute before dinner," Scott heard his father, the voice coming from the top of the stairs, announce.

"Shit! Shit! Shit!" Scott said, trying to guide the tiny ridges along the side that he had to line up with tiny little tongues that further popped in and locked the false bottom section securely into place. Nothing seemed to be working.

As he struggled with the false bottom, he could hear his father's footsteps coming down the stairs. The one saving grace was that his father walked terribly slowly due to his one bad leg, but the rhythmic two-toned thumb of

his one normal shoe, the other built-up heavy Franken-
stein monster shoe pattern sounded, to Scott, like the
rising anxiety-inspiring beat of tension music in a movie
like Jaws or a horror flick where the creature was getting
ever closer.

His father had descended at least a half dozen stairs,
before the false bottom settled into the right position and
finally clicked into place.

Scott breathed a sigh of relief as he placed the top
section of the tackle box back inside and closed the lid.

He managed to get himself across the room and over
to his father's toolbox area, pulling out one of the small
cabinets holding a miscellaneous selection of tiny nails,
screws, and bolts, when his father walked in.

"What are you up to, chief?" his father asked. *Chief*
was one of the nicknames he'd regularly called his son
when he was a kid. It had started off as *Chip*, but then it
migrated to either *Chief* or *Sport* or *Boss* or *Partner*. For
a while, during Scott's teen years, he hated whenever his
father used those terms. Now, though, that he was a little
bit older, hearing his father calling him *Chief* was somehow comforting – something that seemed of definite
importance, particularly now that he'd learned his father
was keeping something rather odd from his family.

"Oh," Scott said, trying to sound casual. "I just need a
sharp object to pop open the hard drive on my laptop."

He proceeded to start explaining some of the technology about the problem he'd been having earlier, knowing
full well that his father would begin to fade out, stop paying attention to his computer-babble. Sure, the man had

been proud that his son was so knowledgeable about computers, but he'd never been interested in hearing him talk about it.

As Scott watched his father's face fade into the standard bored look he got when Scott spoke about computers, Scott wondered if that, too, had been a mask, something kept from the rest of the world, like those strange and intriguing technological devices squirreled away in his father's tackle box.

Chapter Eleven

Today

"Aw, shit, Gary," Scott said. "Not you too!"

Before Scott could do anything, Gary lunged forward, his hands closing around Scott's throat.

Scott reached up and tried to pry Gary's fingers away from their crushing grip on his throat. They both stumbled backwards as Scott simultaneously tried to back away and out of the tight clasp his friend had on his throat.

The back of Scott's legs hit the black leather couch, preventing him from moving back any more.

Scott dug his fingernails into the backs of Gary's hands, but his friend didn't respond to the pain, acted as if nothing were wrong. Gary choked and gasped as the hands closed tighter on his throat.

Managing to slip a couple of fingers from his right hand between Gary's hand and his throat, Scott pulled hard. It brought a bit of relief, but he still couldn't breathe. He again pushed back, and this time they both fell, Gary falling on top of Scott onto the couch.

As they fell, Gary's grip lessened enough for Scott to get his fingers wedged in deeper between his friend's hand and his throat. He pried the hand further away, Scott could again breathe.

"Gary, please don't do this!" Scott gasped.

"You cannot evade us! We will stop you!" Gary said in that same monotone voice, his glassy eyes fixated completely on Scott, barely blinking or showing any emotion.

Scott squirmed and struggled, his right hand further prying Gary's one hand off his throat, his left hand trapped between their bodies against Gary's chest.

As Gary pressed down and struggled against Scott, his breath blew into Scott's face. There was something on Gary's breath, a strange and powerful mothball-like scent. It made Scott's eyes water and he turned his head away from the blast of fetid air.

The distraction from the terrible smell loosened Scott's grip on his friend's hand, and Gary managed to get a tighter hold back onto his throat. Scott was feeling himself begin to fade.

They rocked back and forth on the couch for a few more seconds, with each rock, Scott managed to twist his arm and hand, so he could finally press the palm of his hand against Gary's chest. With an additional back and forth rocking, he also managed to get his elbow against the hard back of the couch.

Figuring he was less than ten or so seconds from "lights out" Scott made one final struggle. With a desperate push of his elbow and against Scott's chest, they both tumbled off the side of the couch and onto the tiled floor, this time with Scott coming down on top of Gary.

Gary didn't let go of Scott's throat as he fell, seeming to completely lack the self-preservation instinct most people might have of putting out an arm to break their fall.

Instead, he kept his hands firmly in the choke-hold on Scott's throat – which was very likely the only thing that saved Scott.

As he went down, Gary's head went first, and the weight of the two men falling was absorbed mostly by the back of his cranium.

Unconscious from the concussion, Gary's hands went slack from Scott's throat and his arms dropped to the ground.

Gasping, Scott knelt over his friend and sucked in the glorious air he had been prevented from pulling in just seconds earlier. He couldn't get away. Gary was laying there, unmoving, his eyes closed, and Scott was terrified that his friend's eyes would snap open and he would reach up and begin choking him again, like in a scene from a horror movie. But despite his fear, he couldn't do anything other than kneel over his friend and keep pulling in lungful after lungful of sweet air.

"Jesus, Gary." Scott finally gasped. "What happened?"

He begin to get up, wondering if Herb and the security guard had been close enough to hear the scuffle. Gary and Scott hadn't been loud at all, except maybe for the fall to the floor and the loud smack of the back of Gary's head. But considering the size of the building and how far they were likely away, he doubted they'd heard a thing.

But he still needed to get away before they came back.

He stood and stepped over to the door.

As he was reaching for it, the knob turned, and from the other side of the door, Herb's voice in unison with the security guard, blended together that now familiar mono-tonic drone of words: "You won't get away. You cannot evade us!"

Chapter Twelve

Four-and-a Half Years Ago

Scott was sitting at the diner table across from the client that had attracted him to the meeting. Despite the delays from his father's surgery, the meeting was still happening, and for that reason, Scott was at a state of unease that he usually didn't face when meeting with a client.

Normally he was confident and somewhat cocky in his approach. The clients needed him more than he needed them, and he could easily command a premium dollar for his services. He could be picky about whom he chose to work with, he could dictate the terms of the relationship.

But, because of the lack of control on his side, the continued delays inflected on the meeting prior to it happening, thanks to the delays at the hospital for his father's surgery, Scott's position of power and authority had been undermined.

The client, upset and angry over the delays, was in the position of power.

Scott was in an undermined position.

And he wasn't used to that at all.

So he was already off guard, a little set back, when his cell phone rang.

"Sorry about that," Scott said, lifting the phone up to flick off the ringer while simultaneously glancing down at the screen to see who was calling. It was a Sudbury area number, one he didn't know, but it was an exchange Scott recognized as being from the hospital.

"You're not answering that," the client barked at him, his cheeks fleshed red, his jowls quivering like a bowl of translucent pink gelatin. "After dicking me around all morning, you're not going to answer that."

Scott looked back at him, wondering at the chances he would be able to make the initial revenue this job had initially promised.

The client, his voice louder, reached out and placed his hairy, thick-knuckled hand over top of Scott's, the one holding his cell phone. "You answer that fucking phone and we're done."

This was a lot of money. Scott looked at him, at his beady little blue-grey eyes, bunched closely together under the thick mono-brow that crossed his forehead. That single caveman-esque eyebrow would have been the man's most striking feature if it weren't for the large bulbous nose. It had obviously been broken multiple times, and it carried a deep red-blue hue, the color associated with years of heavy and abusive drinking.

It was early afternoon and Scott could already smell rye on the man's breath.

He couldn't be more than in his mid-forties, but the man looked to be pushing sixty.

Sitting there, realizing he'd likely already lost the job, Scott hated the man with virtually every single fiber of his being. And, for the first time since he'd started his career as a hacker, he hated this pandering he'd had to do to people like this client; to the dregs and lowest common denominators of society.

He hated himself, the path his life was on, the dealings that were a regular part of his life.

It was a strange awakening to suddenly have dawn on him, all while the phone vibrated in his hand beneath the large clenched first of this client he had so eagerly sought to travel such a great distance in order to be with and woe.

Enough, Scott thought.

"I have to get this," Scott said, angrily pulling his hand from under the client's meaty fist and sliding his thumb across the screen to unlock it for the phone call, lifting the phone to his ear.

"You're done. I'm done," the client said, standing from the table, his chair scraping loudly against the floor as he rose.

"This is Scott," he said into the phone, staring down the client.

"Scott. It's Mom." Her words were anxious, loaded with emotion and panic. Suddenly, the angry client receding back through the diner, and virtually everything else surrounding Scott vanished.

"What is it?"

"It's Dad," She said, and then tried to say something more, but she couldn't force the words through. She started crying.

Scott dropped his phone hand down to the table and stared at the numbers, the numbers of the hospital, the ones he hadn't recognized but figured he'd know based on the exchange.

He stared at the phone, the sounds of his mother sobbing flowing up to his ears.

His father hadn't made it.

He glanced back at the client, watched him stomp out the front door, then looked back down at the phone.

His mother's voice punched through the silence and the sudden ringing in his ears. "Scotty? Are you there?"

"Shit! Shit! Shit!"

Chapter Thirteen

Today

"Shit! Shit! Shit!" Scott said, pulling his hand away from the door handle he had just been reaching for, as if the handle had suddenly started glowing with a white-hot intensity. "What the hell can I do now?"

He looked away from the twisting knob and glanced back at the unconscious and prone body of his friend Gary. Gary was still out.

But for how long?

"Think, think, think," Scott said, pacing back and forth in front of the door. "I haven't had a second to think here. Can't a guy catch a break?"

As if in response, the vent kicked in again, throwing a blast of stifling heat into his face.

Damn heat vent, he thought. This first aid room was not climate controlled (or, at least, vent-controlled), the way that Gary's work area had been. Something also began to itch at his mind -- Gary, the vent – his sudden change in behavior – when he took a closer look at the large opening above him

The vent!

It was wide enough for him to crawl into it.

A way to escape.

He could climb up and into the vent and get away.

On the other side of the door he heard a set of keys jangling.

Shit, he thought. Of course the security guard had a set of keys to every room in this place. It was just a matter of seconds before he got the door open and it was game over for Scott.

Scott looked around the room, his eyes falling onto the couch. A plan started to develop in his mind.

He stepped over top of Gary, grabbed his one arm and one leg and slid the prone body to the back of the room. Then he lifted the one end of the couch and dragged it in front of the door, wedging the high hard back of the couch under the door knob. About seven feet long, it covered not only the door but about a foot and a half on both sides.

Scott then grabbed at the metal cabinet on the side of the room, and, pulling forward, managed to rock it back and forth until it tipped over and slammed down hard on the floor. It was heavy and laid on the floor less than half an inch in front of the couch.

Stepping onto the couch, Scott was pleased with the two purposes it would serve – it, and the heavy cabinet lodged in front of it, would make it harder for Herb and the security guard to get door to open once they unlocked it; and it would also allow him the height needed to get into the vent itself.

Outside, a key slipped into the lock. There was the sound of jostling, but the door didn't unlock. More jangling of keys.

He hasn't found the right key yet, Scott marveled.

Standing on the couch, Scott quickly surveyed the vent grate. It was screwed into the ceiling with a pair of Philips head screws. He reached up and pulled down hard on the vent grate, relaxing his legs to let his body's full weight add to the downward force. Not designed for to withhold a man's weight, the metal bent and one of the screws popped off. The screw clattered to the floor.

Scott paused to look down at Gary again to see that his friend was still out of it where he had been dragged. He then stepped onto the back of the couch as he heard another key slide into the lock. Still no luck, fortunately for Scott.

He pulled the backpack off of his right shoulder and threw it up inside the vent. The he was able to get his right forearm inside the vent and with his left hand grasping the ceiling. From that position, Scott was able to slowly pull himself up and partially into the vent.

His feet swung back and forth as he tried to wiggle a better sense of leverage, pull just a bit more of his upper body inside the vent.

His right shoulder and upper chest propped inside the vent, Scott's feet kept swinging wildly as he managed to gain another inch. Then another, and another.

His mind projected images of high school gym class and the fact that he could never pull himself more than a few feet up the rope from the ever-popular sitting position. Despite the urging of the gym teacher and the fact that the entire class was watching, Scott had never been able to go up more than those first couple of feet.

Mark Leslie

Other kids in the class crawled up the rope as easily as they might ascend a set of stairs, almost like they had been bitten by radioactive spiders. But each year, when it was his turn in that gym class, Scott went up a few feet and then his body, shaking uncontrollably from the strain on his muscles, simply let go and fell back down onto the gym mat, completely defeated and winded and not caring one bit that everyone in the class was laughing at his expense.

Despite believing he had been giving it his all, that he had been putting every possible bit of effort into those gym rope climb attempts, Scott now knew better.

With the result being capture and death rather than mere teenage humiliation, additional resources of strength, power and motivation could be tapped into.

Sliding his entire body into the vent, Scott could hear the sound of yet another key sliding into the lock.

Holy shit, Scott said. *Doesn't the guard remember which key is which?*

No matter, he thought. It's a good thing for me that he's having trouble with it.

Shoving the backpack ahead of him, Scott wormed his way further into the vent. It was dark, dusty and extremely hot. He could see that the vent moved off to the left, to the right, and straight ahead.

No time to think this through, Scott thought, and immediately started crawling down the vent to the left, which would, according to his calculations, take him over top of the 2nd floor kitchen.

Behind him, he heard Herb and the security guard utter the monotonic phrase again, the jiggling of more keys. He kept crawling, seeing if he could put as much distance between himself and the vent opening before they made it into the first aid room. Herb did, after all, have a gun.

Scrambling through the dark, Scott realized it wasn't completely pitch dark inside the vent because of the light that shot up through various openings every few feet. Through them, he could hear the two men continuing to slam against the door, jangle the keys, and occasionally bleating out their threatening lines.

Doing his best to make as little noise as possible while scrambling through the vent, Scott finally made it to the corner at the back of the office. He turned right, knowing he was heading overtop of the same hallway he had first come running down.

As he turned, the sounds of Herb and the guard were harder to make out. He could detect the jangling of the keys, the repeated same four words of "you cannot evade us" sometimes peppered with "you won't get away" and other times with "we will stop you."

Sliding past the short branch that led to the area over Gary's work area, Scott was again reminded of the manner by which Gary had managed to block the airflow in his area.

He was curious as to whether or not the vent had something to do with the behavior of Herb, the guard and Gary; particularly since Gary hadn't seen to shift and morph until he was directly under the vent in the closed first aid room.

Could that be it? Scott wondered, continuing to crawl forward. It was, at least, one theory on why Gary, when he'd been sitting at his workstation, was entirely himself, entirely normal – and that it wasn't until he had been away from the unique environment he had hacked that he slipped into that glassy-eyed state.

No, he told himself. It might first make sense, but that couldn't be it. "I've been breathing the very same air," he whispered. "And I haven't been affected."

He kept crawling forward, heard a loud thump echo from somewhere behind him, figuring that the security guard had finally located the right key, had twisted the lock open and they'd slammed against the door, only to have it hit against the couch and metal cabinet.

Scott figured he had less than a minute before they were able, using their combined force, to get the door open enough to see the entire room, realize he wasn't hiding behind the door, and spot the open vent grate and realize where he had gone.

Moving a bit faster, as quickly as he was able, Scott continued scrambling forward in the vent.

Damn, he thought, considering the fact that, running down the corridor below took a few thirty to forty seconds at best; but crawling along that same length of space seemed to take infinitely longer.

He wasn't sure where, exactly he was heading, wondering if he'd come to another main intersection, and perhaps one that led to another floor. He wondered if he might be able to crawl up or perhaps slide down, or whether he'd get to a branch too thin for an adult male to navigate.

When he got to what he figured was the halfway point of the long corridor, he heard the distinct sounds of foot-steps coming from below.

Damn. They must have figured it out.

Less than a foot in front of him, the vent shaft shot off to the left and the right in a two-way intersection.

A gunshot, muffled like before, the sound less of the small explosive of gunfire, and more like that metallic thwacking of a ruler on a desktop rang out. A small bead of light from the gunshot hole appeared in the metal.

He stared at it for a second, realizing what was hap-pening.

"Shit!" he muttered, and scrambled forward quickly, passing over the gunshot area when a second shot rang out. Something burned on the side of his left leg and he realized he must have been shot, that Herb was likely walking under the vent and taking shots at it, hoping to score a direct hit.

Scott shuffled to the intersection and headed right to-ward the center of the building, the burning sensation on his left leg less concerning than the thought of taking a bullet in the belly.

Another shot fired.

Scott scrambled forward, terrified that Herb would start firing further in the direction Scott was moving, and didn't even notice the floor of the vent disappearing from below him.

Before he realized what was happening, he was tumbling head first in the dark straight down the vertical section of the vent shaft.

Chapter Fourteen

Four-and-a-Half Years Ago

"Natural causes?" Scott yelled out in such a loud voice that he even startled himself. "This is bullshit!"

The coroner, Dr. Mikhail Charuk, sat propped on a little round stool across from Scott and didn't even blink at the harshly delivered words. They were in a small room, the same room that a patient would consult with a doctor in. And Charuk, a Sudbury coroner, ran this service out of the same office he ran his medical practice.

After years of seeing Coroners portrayed on television cop shows, Scott was a bit perturbed to find the Coroner assigned to his father's death was not some eccentric weirdo clutching a ham sandwich in one hand while poking at the edge of a nasty raised edge of flesh on the end of a bloody wound, cracking off-color jokes and spewing out observations that both confused and turned the stomach at the same time, but rather a doctor who looked pretty much like every other doctor Scott had ever encountered.

The Coroner's office was called in because in all cases where a patient dies in either a surgery or a recovery room, an autopsy and investigation has to be completed

Mark Leslie

as part of the due diligence required by the hospital insurance board.

Charuk had just relayed his findings on the investigation into Lionel Desmond's death. He was obviously used to delivering bad news and dealing with upset clients, because the next words he spoke were as calmly and meticulously delivered as all of his previous statements had been.

"Because treating cancer was the underlying reason for your father's surgery," Charuk said, "the findings have to reflect that. Under the circumstances, that is the closest, most logical of the reasons."

"If we didn't treat my father, if he hadn't had the surgery, and if the cancer was allowed to grow and eventually killed him, *that* would be natural causes. I get that.

"But we didn't do that. We sought treatment. He met with medical professionals. They operated on him, removed a kidney, and sewed him back up. Then, less than an hour later, while he was in the recovery room the clips on his renal artery came off. Whether it was from a defect in the clips or the doctor's incompetence, the clips came off. There's nothing natural about that."

"Under the circumstances..." Charuk began in that calm voice.

"I'm talking about the fucking circumstances!" Scott yelled, standing up and slamming the folder on the examining table beside him. "The fucking clips came off! He bled to death! Tell me what's fucking natural about that!"

Charuk paused for a few beats and took a deep breath before he continued. "I understand that you're upset, Mr. Desmond. But in a situation like this, the investigation had to lead back to the root cause, the reason why your father was in surgery in the first place."

"This is utter fucking bullshit!" Scott yelled. "If you're not willing to admit this is either an accident or homicide, then you could at least have offered *undetermined* as the category for his death." Scott had, of course, looked into the situation enough to understand the coroner's role and the five questions they were expected to answer, including the final, most important one, the means by which they died. The categories for that result were: natural causes, accident, homicide, suicide, or undetermined.

"I can see how you might feel this way." Charuk said, his calm poker face unwavering – while that demeanor was likely meant to keep an angry or upset patient or family member stabilized, providing a consistent and comforting platform that they could come back to once their anger, tears or whatever high emotion they were running on had played itself out, all it did was further piss off Scott. "But the reason follows the chain back to the underlying reason why the patient was in the surgery."

"The patient is my fucking father. And he is fucking dead. Thanks either to a quack who should be fucking sued and have his license taken away, or because of a defect in the clips that were used in his surgery.

"THAT is what you were supposed to be determining! THAT is what I was expecting to hear. Not this goddamn fucking bullshit you're spewing!"

"I am sorry you feel this way, Mr. Desmond. And, as I stated, I am truly sorry for your father's loss. But the methodology for determining a death in these circumstances…"

"You can stick your methodology up your ass!" Michael screamed, picking the folder up off of the examining table and opening the door. "Thanks for wasting my time and doing sweet fuck all to look into this!"

"Mr. Desmond…" Charuk said, this time in a partially pleading voice, as if he were talking to an insane person. Scott had to admit that the anger flowing through him, the complete incredulous feeling about what was happening did make him feel insane – insane with rage, insane with disbelief, insane with anger over this situation.

"Go fuck yourself!" Scott said, slamming the door behind him and storming down the hall and out the waiting room past the stares and the fearful looks on the faces of the other patients who had obviously heard most of the exchange – or, at least, Scott's side of the exchange, since he had been the only one yelling.

Leaving through the front door of the office, Scott felt the rage begin to subside, replaced by the tears of rage. He managed to get to his car, unlock the front door, slip inside and close the door behind him before the tears came out full blast.

"Dammit!" he said, pounding his hands on the dashboard and the steering wheel. "This is complete bullshit. They're hiding something, dammit. They're covering something up, and I want to know what it is! Damn, damn, damn, damn, damn!"

Chapter Fifteen

Today

Scott tumbled head-first into the darkness of the vertical section of the shaft, his arms and hands, already in front of him, instinctively embracing for the impact. A quarter of a second into the fall, he worried that this vertical part of the air vent went all the way from the top floor to the bottom and would that a fall from such a height would certainly kill him.

Great, Scott thought. *My fear of heights combined with my fear of the dark merging so beautifully into this perfect end to my life.*

But as his elbows, knees, and heels scraped against the metal walls, he realized this section of the shaft was much more narrow than the horizontal sections he had been navigating through, so he folded his arms together, thrusting his elbows hard against the sides and also spread his legs so that his knees pushed against the sides of the shaft as well.

The initial unbalanced manner by which he pressed against the sides initially bounced him and jostled him within the confines of the metal shaft, and his knees and elbows burned from the friction of the shaft, the ridges of where the pieces of vent joined together tearing into his shirt and cutting him. But he kept the pressure up, pushing out with his arms and legs as much as possible, despite the burning, the pain.

The fear of snapping his neck at the sudden stop at the bottom was a pretty good motivator to help him focus less on the pain and more on just stopping his fall.

He skidded along the shaft for another second or two, the speed of his descent slowing even further.

He pushed out as hard as he could, but the vertical momentum was too much to stop altogether. It did, however, slow him down significantly.

After a few more feet of the reduced speed descent, pressing up against the walls of the shaft, his elbows popped free of the walls on both sides.

The first floor, Scott thought, and thrust both of his arms straight out on each side, feeling the impact of the ledges on both sides digging in to his biceps.

But it was enough of a jolt to his fall that he was able to further spread his legs out and brace them firmly against both sides of the shaft and stop his descent completely.

He hung there, inverted, unmoving, and took a deep breath, trying to figure out how he could twist around and shimmy in to the horizontal section of the shaft without losing his grip and continuing his plummet into the darkness.

Sweat dripped into his eyes as he hung there, catching his breath, trying to work out a quick plan. He could feel a thin line of blood, warm and sticky, running up the back of his leg. It wasn't enough blood to start dripping, but he was certainly aware of it, and of the burning sensation. Although his legs didn't just burn from the spot he figured he'd been shot – they burned in the several spots that had been pressing against the wall in his attempt to slow down the vertical descent.

There was a bit of light coming from off to his right. There was a steady stream of heat blowing up through the shaft, more intense now that his plummet had stopped, and likely further aggravated by the fact that most of the mass of his body was blocking the heat from continuing to rise.

Scott twisted his hips, slowly moving his knees towards his front while pushing the back of his head against the side of the metal shaft. The edges of the horizontal section of the air vent dug deeper into his biceps as he slowly twisted and shifted.

He knew that he couldn't remain suspended there much longer. His arms would eventually give out and he would plummet all the way to the bottom.

So he had to do something a bit risky – he had to tuck in, do a quick twist, lift his left arm out of the shaft to his left, and thrust it into the one to his right; at the same time he had to continue to twist and thrust his legs completely into the opposite horizontal section, so that his body was planking the gap.

He knew that, while perfectly suspended he might stand a chance of holding himself by gripping onto the ledge of metal, even falling the half foot would be too much for him – the slick metal, particularly with him sweating the way he was in the over-heated enclosed heating vent, wouldn't allow him any sort of proper grip. There wouldn't be enough friction to hold himself upright.

Scott flashed back to the scene in *Die Hard* where Bruce Willis's character, John McClane falls down a section of a significantly larger air vent, more akin to the size of an elevator shaft. In the movie he fell a couple of stories before the last two portions of the fingers of both hands end up catching the edge of one of the horizontal sections and completely stop his fall.

It wasn't a matter of physical strength, Scott knew – certainly, McClane was tough enough to hold himself up with just the tips of his fingers for a few seconds – but the issue was simple physics. There's no way that a man in the weight class of almost two hundred pounds would be able to stop such a rapid descent with such a minimal point of contact, the tips of eight fingers. Never mind the speed of his fall and the slickness of the metal itself, but McClane had already been sweating and he was covered with blood.

While McClane had fallen a few stories and still managed the miraculous save, Scott knew that, if he twisted incorrectly, despite having one full arm extended into the horizontal section, the downward pull of his weight would be enough to dislodge him and send him tumbling down the vertical section of shaft again. There was, simply, nothing for him to grasp onto. His fingers couldn't dig into or catch on anything.

He took a deep breath, did the final twist and, with all of his might, pulled his left arm in and shoved it quickly into the same side his right arm was in. At the same time, he tucked, twisted, and pulled his legs in, then immediately thrust his legs back out on the opposite direction with all of his might.

His legs pushed through the horizontal section on the far side, a bizarre feeling to have them meet no resistance after the previous several seconds of intense pressure against the metal sides of the air shaft. A split second later, his hip connected with the bottom of the horizontal section digging into his hip. His arms started to slip as the downward momentum wanted, desperately, to pull him naturally down.

He jammed his elbows against the sides of the shaft and prevented himself from falling.

He hung there, his body planking across the section of vertical shaft, and let out a deep breath.

Then, after a few seconds, he managed to get the tip of his shoe against one of the tiny ridges that connected the sections of the shaft and push his upper body further into the one side. Scrambling with his feet and slowly pulling himself forward with sweaty, slick fingers, he managed to get to a point where his body weight was enough overtop the horizontal section that there was no chance of him being pulled down the vertical section of shaft.

Secure and safe, at least from the fall, he let out another deep breath and rested there, giggling the way John McClane did immediately after surviving a pretty precarious situation in that classic adventure movie. "Eat your heart out, McClane," Scott chuckled in a half sigh, half laugh. "Yippie Kaye Yay!"

Mark Leslie

Chapter Sixteen

Four-and-a-Half Years Earlier

Dr. Citino, the surgeon who had performed the nephrectomy on Scott's father was a difficult man to find any information on, despite all of the manners by which Scott had access to the average person's lives using online databases.

He'd spent hours searching through and hacking various university and hospital databases in order to see what he could find out about the man, but at virtually every stop he made along the digital journey, there was little new or fresh evidence in place.

It was almost, if Scott were to speculate wildly, as if somebody had gone in, within a single system, and entered a basic single paragraph worth of information about the man – like cribbed notes from a Wikipedia entry, the information about Citino that appeared on various websites and in informational databases was almost the exact same word for word.

Citino grew up in a small town in Eastern Ontario, went to Arnprior High School, attended the undergraduate medical program at the University of Ottawa, then moved to Laurentian University where he received his MD. He was single, never married, had no children, and, apart from becoming a surgeon was unremarkable in virtually every possible way. There were only a handful of pictures of him as a student at both institutions as well as in his roll on the staff at the University hospital in Sudbury, where he was an attending physician with a specialty in surgery. There were a few high school pictures of him, but he hadn't been a member of any clubs and thus, apart from a few class photos of him through the years, there were no other images of him from high school.

The man drove a late eighties Ford Taurus, never had a single speeding ticket, parking ticket or accident claim on his vehicle. His criminal record, like his driving record, was untarnished and completely clean. He had a locked Facebook profile – although it was not at all hard for Scott to gain access to his full wall – with a simple photo (one of his staff pictures from his intern days at Laurentian hospital), a handful of friends and less than a dozen updates. Similarly, he had an old neglected and poorly established *MySpace* page with the same photo and a couple of lines of text about him. The only new information there was a line expressing his enjoyment of honkytonk and new country music.

Digging deeper into Citino's medical records on staff, Scott had been able to compile some of the stats on his surgeries. They were, like his driving and criminal records, unblemished in any way – but, like the rest of his life, they were also not at all remarkable in any way either.

Scott had spent several weeks combing through the various records, medical charts and reports in which

Citino was named in any way, whether it had been as his time as a full-fledged surgeon or whether it had anything to do with his time as a medical intern or even med student.

About the only interesting thing Scott had found was, back before medical school, when Citino was an undergrad at the University of Ottawa, he had spent a co-op term on the fourth floor of the Royal Ottawa Mental Health Centre where he had worked as part of the team that had treated Wendel Schmidt, a CSIS agent during his stay at the hospital following a mental breakdown he had incurred.

Scott found himself reading more about Schmidt and his exemplary record as a field intelligence agent, working on special projects and high tech espionage, rather than following up on Citino himself. Time and again, he caught himself following links to information and profile details about Schmidt, and, only after half an hour of falling down another rabbit hole, realized he had gone on a tangent and was reading about the agent's work and experiences, speculation about the top secret program he had been working on which caused the breakdown, instead of going back to look at Citino.

What does it say about a man's intrigue and presence in society when one of the most interesting things you can say about him has nothing to do with him, and everything to do with a particular patient he treated – or, in the case of Citino, he wasn't even the lead physician, but rather an intern charged with doing some of the menial tasks and examinations.

Taking no chances that he would miss anything, Scott dug deep on all of the patients and surgeries Citino had performed – he only realized what he'd been hoping to find when nothing came up. He'd been expecting and hoping, perhaps, to find a pattern of carelessness or previous errors and mistakes in surgery. He'd been hoping he could find some sort of evidence that would prove Citino had a history of errors, a history of botched surgeries, a history perhaps, even, of medical malpractice suits held against him – anything that would allow Scott the opportunity to prove his negligence and hold him responsible, legally, for his father's death.

But there was nothing there. No errors, no malpractice suits in which he was the main attending surgeon, no skeletons in any of the closets.

The man's credit history was pretty straight-line and standard. He'd had student loans and paid them off in a timely fashion, particularly considering the incredible costs he had incurred going to medical school. But his payments were always on time, as were his credit card statement payments. He made the occasional car repair or furniture or appliance purchase on his VISA, and either paid the entire balance the day the statement came in or, with larger purchases, made the regular monthly payment plus additional funds in order to bring the balance down more quickly. But he never held a balance for more than six months, and, for the most part, kept a zero balance on his single credit card.

Pretty much the only interesting financial transaction that Scott could find had to do with the small house on

Ramsey Lake that Citino owned. He'd bought it a few years after becoming a surgeon, at about the time his loans were pretty close to being paid off. He'd made the small five percent down-payment required and paid the bank in rapid bi-weekly payments. Once every six months he would make an additional lump sum payment on the mortgage – and that's where Scott became confused. The money had come from a savings account Citino had set up, an account towards which he regularly deposited ten percent of each of his paychecks.

But, when Scott looking into the history of that savings account, he found there were additional funds trickling in to the account from an outside source. Getting to the source had been challenging, but Scott found they were coming from an offshore account in the name of an Alexander Citino, the surgeon's uncle on his father's side. According to medical records, Alexander Citino had died three decades earlier, and, childless, had bequeathed his accumulated wealth to his one nephew, Maurice.

When Scott dug back deep enough, he saw that, throughout Citino's school and medical career, the funds had been steadily coming in. Nothing spectacular, but enough to make a small positive difference.

What was strange was that, after a decade and a half of the same monthly fund – Two hundred and fifty dollars – being deposited into Citino's account, at about the time the surgeon had purchased his house, the funds changed such that every second month two thousand and five hundred dollars was being deposited instead of two hundred and fifty.

Scott couldn't figure out why or how the deposit pattern had suddenly changed, but, recognizing this matter likely had nothing to do with Citino's competency as a physician or surgeon, he let the matter go.

He didn't just look into Citino's life. He spent several weeks uncovering as much information as he could about the surgery itself, the surgery's history, how often incidents like his father's had occurred, who the manufacturer of the clips were, what surgery's they were used on, as well as a host of other medical instruments and supplies that the same company produced.

There was nothing that came up in his research that suggested to him a pattern he could use to lay the blame for his father's death on the manufacturer.

He'd been about to look back into Citino's uncle, to determine where the money had come from, when an article in the Ottawa Citizen popped up mentioning the surgeon.

Sudbury Surgeon Presumed Dead In Horrific Accident

Dr. Maurice Citino, a Sudbury region surgeon who grew up in the Ottawa valley and attended University of Ottawa, was driving along the Rocliffe Parkway early Sunday morning when his vehicle lost control, crashed through the guardrails and plunged into the Ottawa River.

Emergency crews were called from a nearby residents reported the sounds of screeching tires and the crash. The resident, who asked not to be named, said that he was just letting his dog back in from the back yard, when he heard the noise.

"At first I thought it was teens racing," the resident said, explaining that teens often used the parkway as a race zone, trying to recreate scenes out of *The Fast & The Furious*. "Because I heard the roaring engines and screeching tires. But then I heard the crash. I let the dog in, closed the door and ran through the house to the front door to see what was going on.

"At first I couldn't see nothing," the resident continued. "The parkway was empty and there were no cars in sight at all. I thought I might see a car up against the rails, which isn't all that uncommon around that hairpin turn. But then, when the clouds shifted and the moonlight shone through, I could see the broken guard rail. That's when I knew."

The resident reported that this was the third time he had seen an accident like this in the five years he has lived in the home.

"Sure, there are a lot of cars that hit the rail. Maybe one every second week. But only three so far have broken through. He was driving real fast. That I could hear before the crash."

Ottawa Fire & Rescue were the first to arrive, and they deployed a team to descend the cliff, looking for survivors. "Sometimes cars get lodged in the trees on the side of the cliff," Lieutenant Mike Lazarius explained. "But there was nothing lodged in any of the foliage that we could see with our flashlights, so we started to make our way down."

The car wasn't found until almost two hours later, just as the sun was coming up. Lazarius and his team located the car completely submerged about half a kilometer down-stream from the crash site. The car was empty. No survivors, nor any victims.

"Those waters move pretty quickly this time of year," Lazarius said. "If somebody was in that car and managed to get out, it was unlikely they would have been able to fight the current enough to get back to shore. They most likely would have been carried further downstream and into the rapids." Lazarius was referring to the rapids located another hundred yards downstream from where the vehicle was found.

The crew dragged the water and also scouted along the shore and through the trees of the cliff until mid-day on Sunday, but no bodies were found.

While the occupants of the car could not be determined for certain, police did confirm that the vehicle was registered to Dr. Maurice Citino, a Sudbury area surgeon. Citino was registered at an academic conference at the University of Ottawa, the school he received his undergrad degree from.

According to colleagues and the conference registration records, Citino arrived in town two nights earlier and was scheduled to do a presentation on Monday morning. But he never arrived and has not been seen since.

Citino was assumed to be in the vehicle, as the sole oc-cupant of the car at the time of the crash and is presumed dead. No next of kin have been identified.

Police are asking anybody who might have been in con-tact with Citino on Sunday evening, or anybody who might be able to provide information helpful to their investigation to contact them at 613-555-5469.

As the week went on, Scott found a few other articles referring to the crash, along with a follow-up series of the dangers of stunt driving, an account of the history of crashes that had taken place on the Rockcliffe Parkway over the years, and a plea, by a local residents, to install speed-calming measures on three different areas of the Parkway that were prone to similar accidents.

Citino was only mentioned, very briefly, in a couple of follow up articles. No new information was provided, simply the fact that Citino was still missing and presumed dead and that no bodies were recovered.

The Sudbury area paper ran a couple of short articles about the surgeon missing, with a request from the local police detachment to have anybody who might be able to assist in the search for the missing surgeon to contact them.

Another week later, Scott found a memorial post up on the Laurentian University Hospital website. It was a simple picture, one of the three staff photos he had previously been able to find of Citino, and this one, in Scott's opinion, being one of the less attractive pictures of the man, with a few lines of text.

IN MEMORIUM, the article read, and then mentioned Citino had been a surgeon at the hospital for ten years, had been a graduate of Laurentian's medical school, and did not have any family.

The whole thing threw Scott into a depression.

His father's death had overwhelmed him, for sure.

But Citino's death, and the utter lack of any lasting legacy, seemed even harder on Scott.

Sure, he had originally been looking at the surgeon to try to lay some sort of blame on him for his father's death. Citinio had become a focal point, something that Scott could channel a huge degree of his anger, resentment and hatred towards. Looking into Citino's past, trying to find something – anything – on him that could lay the groundwork for blaming him, holding him responsible for Lionel Desmond's death, kept Scott going, gave him the forward momentum to keep going in the face of the incredible angst and pain he'd felt with his father's loss.

But when Citino died like that, completely unexpectedly, it had a bizarre and unique effect on him.

Scott mused about Citino's unremarkable life, at the fact that this fifty-eight year old surgeon, somebody who had achieved something unique, a medical degree, a life dedicated to the Hippocratic Oath, to healing others, could be gone so quickly, so easily, and with virtually nothing to show for it.

The loss of Scott's father happened unexpectedly and had hit Scott powerfully. But he had been so consumed with anger and wanting to blame someone, that he had allowed his pursuit of investigation to keep him going, keep him from thinking about the mortality in front of him.

But when Citino also died, Scott had no choice but to reflect back on that, reflect on death, on the finality of it all. Sure, Lionel Desmond had his wife and his son; he had some sort of legacy, people who would remember him, and cherish him and, in the manner Scott had been doing these past weeks, fight on his behalf. But Citino had nobody – no family, no friends. He had lived a life dedicated mostly to his profession as a doctor, as a surgeon.

Scott's father had fishing, a passion that had kept him going beyond work, given him something to purse in his spare time. Citino didn't seem to have any hobbies, any passions outside of work.

All he had, it seemed, was work, was his job.

And when he died, there was nothing.

Scott couldn't help but reflect on his own life, on his own situation, on the manner by which he had pursued the things he had gone after.

He enjoyed the computer skills he had perfected. And he made a significant amount of money doing the black market work he had done. He had become known through hacker circles as a proficient expert, someone who could be turned to perform remarkable tasks, hack into systems that nobody else seemed capable of.

He was, by many different measures, at the top of his field.

But beyond his hacking skills, beyond his reputation, beyond the money he could command for the tasks, the selective manner by which he was in such high demand that he could easily turn down three out of every five jobs that came his way, what did Scott really have?

Nothing.

Sure, the money he made had allowed him to spend almost a full month of investigating his father's death, of taking no jobs, not needing to answer any phone calls, any emails. He had enough money to comfortably live on while he pursued this investigation. He had enough money put away, in fact, to allow him to continue to live comfortably for at least another four months while pursuing his quest.

But to what end?

What did Scott really have?

He had work, he had his skills, and he had money.

But that was it.

Like Citino, that was pretty much all he had.

He spiraled into a deep depression for several days, continually speculating about what his own obituary might say about him. Would anyone even write one for him?

He doubted it.

Then then thought back to all of the times his father had reflected on Scott's grandfather's life.

Sure, the man had died quite young. But he had been a war hero; he had brought his family something to be proud of. His life, though short-lived, had served a greater purpose.

Scott's father had never gone anywhere without carrying around a picture of his father. He even kept those secret photos of his Dad locked away in his tackle box.

Lionel Desmond carried the legacy, the memory of his father everywhere he went.

He had, it seemed, made much of his life based on the message, the legacy, the example his father had set for him.

Scott reflected back on the words his father had spoken to him once about his grandfather.

"I never really knew him all that well," Lionel Desmond had said as they sat by the campfire one quiet evening after a marathon day of fishing. He'd had one too many beer and was a bit chattier than he normally would be. Scott had sat quietly as his father had been reflecting about his old man "But it feels as if he is always with me, you know? I keep that picture of him in my wallet and I look at it at least once every day.

"And every decision I make, every choice about the things that I do, I look at his picture, I look at this distinctive eyes, and I wonder: *What would you say to me about this, Dad? What would you do in my position?* And then I know what to do, I know what my next step is.

"I never really knew him, but his memory, his legacy guides me every single day."

Scott pulled himself out of the deep dark funk, out of the terrible depression he had found himself spiraled down into, when he realized that, like his father, he could do the same thing.

Scott's grandfather had served his country, had dedicated his life to a greater cause. Heck, he had given his life for a greater cause. That example had been a guiding principle for Scott's father.

And it could be a guiding principle for Scott.

He decided, then and there, to stop using his computer and hacking skills for his personal gain, in the quest for money or for hacking just for hacking's sake, for the joy of being able to break or crack a system.

He could put his powers to good use. He could serve a greater good.

From that point on, Scott stopped accepting hacking work. Instead, he embraced the knowledge that all of the things he had learned, all of the skills he had accumulated, all of the systems he had been able to hack, could be put to great use.

He could use those powers for good.

People could benefit from the things Scott knew, the systems he understood, the loopholes he had been able to find and exploit.

From that day on, Scott turned his life around.

All thanks to that quiet and mysterious death of the surgeon who had killed his father.

Within a few weeks, he had started to contract himself out as a security expert, a firewall inspection coordinator, an internet security consultant.

He didn't make nearly as much money as the illegal activities had netted him.

But it felt good.

He ended up keeping the same photo his father had carried around in his wallet, the picture of his grandfather in his army uniform, in his own wallet.

And, while doing the good work, working the type of role that his father and his grandfather would be proud, something that would ensure Scott would leave this world a better place than it had been when he started, he continued to use those hacking skills for one selfish purpose – although it was not nefarious in any way.

On the contrary.

He still didn't believe or understand the circumstances leading to his father's death.

He simply couldn't accept the situation the way it had occurred.

He knew, and his gut told him this in no uncertain terms, that there was something more to his father's death; there was something deeper than could be seen on the surface, something Scott knew he could uncover if he just kept at it.

And that became his hobby, his passion, his pursuit – the thing he did every single day when he wasn't working, wasn't dedicating his work time to helping companies protect himself from the type of hacker he used to be.

And it felt good.

Really good.

Chapter Seventeen

Today

Scott laid inside the air vent for what felt like at least one full minute before he was able to properly catch his breath. The heat blowing through the ventilation shaft didn't help matters. It filled his throat, making the air he was trying to swallow seem thick and dry. But he did his best to take deep gulps of air.

The throbbing burning sensation in Scott's leg where he'd been shot intensified. It had all but disappeared during the time he'd been *plummeting to his imminent death*.

Maslow's Hierarchy of Needs, Scott bemused. Who would be worried about a gunshot wound when there was a more immediate life-preserving concern at hand?

He wondered, like he had back before he'd climbed into the vent, if there was something circulating through the air vent that might account for the behavior of Herb, the security guard and Gary.

Given the manner by which Gary had rerouted the air vent near his work area, it did seem to make some sort of sense. After all, it hadn't been until shortly after Gary had left the cocooned area of his workspace that he had morphed into the hive-mind mentality that had taken over Herb and the guard.

"This is like *Invasion of the Body Snatchers*," Scott mused aloud, imagining that wonderfully horrific scene from the 1978 remake with Donald Sutherland where Sutherland's character appears in front of the heroine who momentarily believes all will be okay, before Sutherland stops, raises an arm and thrusts a finger at her and lets out a high pitched scream – the surest indication that this is not the man she knew, but, rather, an alien imposter in his guise.

Only, Scott figured, this wasn't an alien pod invasion. This was something that affected people, took them over, controlled their behavior. He had witnesses the sudden and disturbing change in Gary right before his eyes.

And the only thing that Scott could figure would have caused the change was some sort of airborne matter.

It was the one decent control Scott could figure.

Gary had been the only normally behaving person Scott had seen. Everyone else that morning, well, all two of them at least, had been out to kill Scott. The only other person he'd seen had been the person coming up to the second floor from the first floor, likely a new arrival. He hadn't been sure who that was, just that it was a male and he was wearing blue jeans.

Blue Jeans seemed to be walking normally, not at all behaving like Herb or the guard, or the way Gary had once he had been outside the controlled air vent area, at least.

Perhaps that was because Blue Jeans had just entered the building and perhaps it took the airborne virus or whatever it was, a few minutes to get into a person's airway and "take them over."

It all fell into place, and made sense – not that Scott understand any of the *hows* or the *whys* or the *whos* as in who was behind this – except for one small matter.

Why had Scott not been affected by the airborne infecting agent?

It was almost as if everybody was working against Scott, simultaneously working from the same playbook.

He recalled that when Herb and the guard were searching outside the door, they hadn't even spoken a single word to one another. It was as if they were in contact with one another's mind – like there was some sort of telepathic connection between the two of them.

Not to mention the fact that they spoke in unison.

You won't get away. You cannot evade us!

Gary, too, had been following that exact same script.

So, what, then, was different about Scott?

Why had he not been affected?

It only stood to reason that the reason he wasn't affected might just be because he was the intended target. Yes, maybe that was it. Perhaps he – Scott – was the reason why these people were turned into some sort of mind-controlled zombies and had come after him.

But why?

And who was behind it?

It's not as if Scott had been involved in anything illegal. It had been almost five years since he had done any contract work for people whose purposes had been nefarious and whose activities had been, if not outright illegal, then at least on the periphery of the law. But perhaps it had taken this amount of time to find Scott. It's not as if he left any sort of easy to track digital trail behind wherever he went. And, when he had turned his life around, he had completely abandoned the false name and hacker identity that he used for his work.

It would have taken a significant investment of time and the right people – i.e., whose skill at least matched if not superseded Scott's own hacker ability – in order to trace Scott down. Not that it would be impossible, but he failed to understand just how and why, and who would not only be capable of that, but would even bother.

Besides, it would be one thing to track Scott down, show up at his apartment in the middle of the night to break his legs or put a bullet in his head while he was sleeping. It was quite another to introduce an airborne virus capable of controlling people and turning them into homicidal robots.

Who wanted Scott Desmond dead not only that badly, but in such a way that the death would be difficult to explain or trace back to the originator?

And, almost as importantly, why?

What the hell had Scott done to warrant such a bold and unique attack?

He started crawling away from the vertical shaft, towards a spot about ten feet away where the light shone in from the open vent grate below, the questions rotating through his mind without any sort of answer coming to him.

Scott needed to get to an area with more light, so he could inspect where he'd been shot in the leg, see how bad the damage actually was. Sure, it burned, and he knew it was bleeding. He could feel where the blood had seeped into his jeans, where it had dripped up his legs while he'd been hanging upside down.

But he couldn't feel the bullet inside him.

Is that because there's no bullet there, and the bullet had grazed him? Or was it because one didn't feel a bullet, that it entered with a white hot intensity of a hot knife cutting through butter. Or maybe because it exited the other side of his leg.

No, he thought. I'd feel burning on the other side, where it exited. Or, more likely, it would have struck or shattered the bone. And that would have hurt more than a simple burning.

It's most likely, he figured, that the bullet was either lodged in a somewhat superficial manner in the meat of his leg, or perhaps it did just graze him, causing some fleshy damage, but not nearly as bad as actually being shot.

Not that he would know, of course. It's not as if a person got shot every day.

Heck, it's not as if most people had ever been shot at.

And, until this morning, Scott had been a gunfire recipient virgin.

Footsteps could be heard on the concrete floor below, so he stopped just shy of the edge and peered over carefully.

There was nobody within sight of the grate from the angle he was looking down. He could make out the first floor photocopier, which was at the midway point in the large mostly open office space. Unlike the second floor, which had a series of offices running in two spots in the center of the room, the first floor had a few offices along both walls and an open central area where row after row of simple Ikea-style rectangular desks were aligned for the call agents who worked on the first floor.

The large open office area had somewhat reminded Scott of the photos of a large city's newsroom, a sea of desks as far as the eye could see, and swarms of people sitting at them, leaning over to converse with their neighbors, a phone in one hand, some sort of printed documentation in the other.

It had been a collaborative work area – something Digi-Life used in their marketing campaign, offering the fact that while their systems operated 24/7 and the advanced program algorithms worked tirelessly to find their clients the best of all possible deals, Digi-Life wasn't just about a digital life – it was about real people, helping other real people, to save money and save time. Agents were on call 24/7 to take their call.

Of course, there was never more than perhaps a single agent here after standard work-day hours. The front-line agents Digi-Life hired were a massive team of third-party call center agents from India; all fully trained to speak in Canadian and American accents and ready to take your Digi-Life call day and night.

The first floor of the Toronto office was where the Tier 2 Digi-Life agents worked, and most of them during a standard nine to five shift. While the outsourced team in India handled the majority of calls, perhaps eighty-five to ninety percent of the incoming queries and calls that could easily be responded to with a series of basic scripts all designed to seem like natural and knowledgeable sales people, these agents handled the customers who needed additional follow-up, whose questions and concerns and needs went beyond what could sate the majority.

Thank goodness for those outsourced agents in India, Scott thought. Because if this floor had been filled with a roomful of agents, they likely all would have been taken over by the airborne virus that had infected Herb, the security guard and Gary. And Scott would never be able to get out.

The footsteps were coming from somewhere to the left, out of earshot.

It sounded to Scott less as if somebody was going about a normal morning routine – dropping stuff off at their desk, turning on their computer, heading over to the kitchen at the back of the first floor in order to get a coffee from the coffee dispenser that ground the coffee fresh for every new serving – and more like they were pacing.

But he knew better.

They weren't pacing.

They were searching.

For him.

He reached into his pocket for his mobile phone in order to check the time. It had been several years since he had worn a watch. Almost ten years, in fact. His parents had bought him one when he graduated from high school, and he had worn it for a few years, but soon fell out of the habit, only wearing it to a few formal occasions, like his University graduation, charity dinners and other corporate events that he had started attending when he took on the more serious consulting role that had led to this gig at Digi-Life. He'd stopped wearing a wristwatch at about the same time he started to carry a mobile phone on him.

It kept the time perfectly, and in sync with a standard time through the mobile company carrier's live connection.

Scott had long bemused the fact that the gesture of checking one's wrist to indicate that something was taking a long time or that you were expected or needed elsewhere soon was soon becoming something that might characterize people from his father's generation; with Scott's generation and, more likely, the one after his, it might just be reaching into one's pocket to pull out a smartphone and glancing at the screen.

He lifted his phone out of his pocket and thumbed the button on the top right to turn it on – he didn't need to unlock it – that simple gesture would trigger the screen saver to pop up, complete with the time, in digital format, to flash near the top of the screen.

Only, when Scott thumbed the button, the screen remained dark. Nothing came on.

He thumbed it again.

Still nothing.

He held the button down, expecting the little fruit icon to appear like it did whenever the device was being powered on or powered down.

Nothing.

He lifted the phone closer to the light coming in from the vent grate, and once the front of the screen caught the shaft of light, Scott could see the hairline crack running down the middle of the screen.

It must have broken in the fall.

Damn!

Funny how not having access to a simple thing like a mobile phone could cause this type of angst – and not merely because of the denied access to email or checking a Twitter or Facebook feed, or even the score of the basketball game; just something as simple as time.

Excuse me, mister. But do you have the time?

Thinking back to what time it had been when Herb called him in to his office, Scott figured it couldn't be more than 7:45 AM. He knew he had less than half an hour before the first floor began to fill with employees, adding to the army of robotic assassins who were after Scott.

Scott listened to the footsteps as they receded towards the back of the office, Scott started crawling toward the front of the office, trying to figure out how he was going to get out of the air vent. With the limited space he had, there was no way he'd be able to kick the vent grate off.

A few feet ahead, the air shaft forked off to the left and the right. At both ends a larger vertical vent grate was visible, but the shaft narrowed down from the rectangular shape he'd been moving through, which was perhaps three feet across and two and a half feet wide and funneled down to a narrower section of rounded pipe, maybe two feet in diameter.

If he hoped to kick the grate off, he'd have to back into that section.

He turned, twisted and shift in the air vent, managing to tuck and pull and twist himself so that his feet were pointed towards the grate opening, and then slowly pushed himself towards it.

It took almost twice as long to move the same distance.

But when he got to the grate, almost eight feet away, he realized he was inside one of the VP's offices. He recognized one of the prints of elk on the wall.

Good, he figured. Those offices were kept locked. Meaning, when someone heard him kicking and rushed over, there'd be a delay in getting inside.

Not that Scott knew what he'd do once he got out of the air vent. Just that he had to get out of it and get out of the building.

He braced himself and kicked hard with both feet.

The vent rattled and shook.

Shit! This would definitely bring somebody coming.

He kicked again. And again. Then, on the fourth kick, the vent went flying off, and he shimmied as quickly as he could out of the opening, having to take his backpack off to fit through the opening. But he managed to keep the backpack with him by looping one of the straps from the top around his right hand.

He lowered himself out the shaft opening and dropped to the floor just as a voice outside the door, a new one, called out.

"You won't get away. You cannot evade us!"

Mark Leslie

Chapter Eighteen

Three Years Earlier

Despite the long hours spent wandering the Exhibition GO station, where Scott had seen his dead father walking around as live and as real as anyone else, he never spotted him again.

"Of course not," Scott mumbled to himself on the third day that he had found himself scouring the area of the platform where he had spotted his father and walking, dejected, back down the platform and towards the parking lot adjacent to the ticket booth area under the elevated section of the Gardiner Expressway. "The man knew how to keep secrets from us his whole life. Of course he wouldn't be stupid enough to go back to the place I had spotted him."

It had most certainly been his father. Scott had been as sure of that as of anything he saw that he'd known for sure.

Confused and unsure where to turn, who to turn to – Scott didn't, after all, really have any friends – he looked up somebody whom he hadn't spoken with in several years. Mr. Prescott. His computer science teacher from high school.

Mark Leslie

He knew that Prescott lived in Toronto and had moved down there after he'd retired from teaching in order to be closer to his daughter and their family. Scott had seen his computer mentor briefly at his father's funeral and learned that Prescott had made the long haul from Toronto up to Sudbury to offer his condolences to Scott and his mother.

So, confused and frustrated and needing someone to talk to, Scott looked up Mr. Prescott's address and phone number. Even if they weren't listed it wouldn't have been hard for Scott to find them. And when he found the listing he grinned at the listing of the man's name.

J. T. Prescott.

He knew that stood for *James Timothy Prescott*.

He also knew that the man went by "Tim" rather than by his first name. This was because it was a family tradition for every male in the Prescott family to be given the name of James. Thus, to eliminate confusion, those men went by their middle names.

Scott knew quite a bit about Mr. Prescott, because they'd spent so much time together. Prescott became more than just a good teacher, more than just the person who existed as a figurehead at the front of the classroom. Prescott had, unlike most of the other teachers Scott had, transcended that odd barrier in place between most students and most teachers.

Scott recalled that odd feeling, when he had first learned of Mr. Prescott's first name. It was odd for students, even in high school, back in Scott's day, at least, to think about their teachers as real people with full names.

For years, the education system had drilled into them that their teachers were Mr. This and Mrs. or Ms. or Madame That.

They never had full names.

They never had lives outside of the classrooms.

To the younger students, the teachers lived only for the classroom and couldn't possibly have a life outside of that calling. The thought of a teacher being just another human, a person like one of your own parents was almost unthinkable.

Every once in a while, of course, there would be a teacher whose child was in the same class. And that threw the myth for a bit of a loop, because suddenly you'd find yourself imagining the teacher with a life, with a family, getting up in the morning, fixing breakfast, making sure everyone was ready for school.

The same mystique was busted whenever Scott might see a teacher out in "the wild" – out in public in the grocery store or at the mall. It would be an awkward moment, seeing the teacher, not in a position of authority, but rather as a normal adult, wandering about the world just like anybody else.

Even in the relationship that Scott had built up with Mr. Prescott, much of the mystique had been held together. Scott knew the man's first and middle names.

But he'd never used the first name.

No, despite the fact he knew that Mr. Prescott used his middle name, Tim, He had even heard other teachers call him that. But he still had always thought of him as Mr. Prescott and not James Timothy Prescott or even Tim, as he was known to his friends.

He called Mr. Prescott and they met at a café in downtown Toronto, where Scott told him everything he had seen that morning.

When he'd finished laying out the details of that morning at Exhibition GO station, Scott started to run down the possibilities he had kept only in the back of his head.

"I don't know what to think, Mr. Prescott. Do you think, perhaps that this could be a long lost twin brother?"

Prescott leaned forward, offered the beaming smile that warmed so many high school students to him within seconds of him entering their first class with him; it was a smile that peeked out playfully from behind the thick Tom Selleck style moustache that would, normally, appear as if his face was meant only for a serious presentation to the world.

"Scott, please, call me Tim. My Dad's name is Mr. Prescott. Cut this guy a little bit of slack, would you? I already feel over the hill, being retired, having passed sixty a few years back, being a grandfather and all that other 'old guy' jazz like seniors discounts, regular prostrate exams and everything.

"If you call me Tim you'll help me feel younger and better about myself. Deal?"

"Deal." Scott smiled. The man's ability to make the person or classroom he was speaking with feel one hundred percent at ease had not been reduced in any way. If anything, it was more refined, stronger, more powerful than before. "So, do you, think, Tim, that the man I saw could be my father's twin brother?"

"It might be possible," Prescott said, looking down into his coffee as he worked through the logic. "But you don't think that the fact he had a twin brother would have come up at all in any conversations or mentioned at any family gatherings over the years?"

"I don't know. Maybe they had a falling out, my dad and his brother. Maybe something so terrible happened that caused a rift between them. Something big; something major. So big that nobody dared mention dad's brother to him. One of those: 'you're dead to me!' sentiments you sometimes hear about."

"That is possible. But what about pictures? You'd mentioned knowing very little about your dad's childhood. But weren't there any pictures of your dad that would include his brother? Wouldn't you have seen any?"

Scott thought back about it. "Well, there weren't all that many pictures of Dad when he was younger. But, you're right. None of them include a brother."

"So the twin brother hypothesis seems unlikely then."

"I don't know. What if the falling out was so bad that my dad destroyed all of the pictures, not wanting to have anything there to remind him of the man."

"Now you're stretching it, Scott. You need to come back to the simpler solution, don't you think?"

Scott took a sip of his coffee, and, even though it was fixed exactly the way he liked it he picked up the glass container of sugar from the center of the table and tipped it over the coffee, sprinkling in another large spoonful. It was a gesture designed to stall, to pause. When Scott looked back up at Mr. Prescott he knew the man knew exactly what he was doing. Prescott raised his bushy black eyebrows high onto his forehead and his playful smile peeked out from under the moustache.

"Okay, so maybe he didn't know his twin brother. Maybe they were separated at birth, and that's why there are no pictures of him."

"Sure, it's a possibility," Prescott said. "And more likely than a rift between two brothers where there is absolutely no evidence or any supporting family information that would suggest a brother existed."

"Okay, so it was a twin brother separated at birth. That could explain what I saw."

"It is possible that your father has a twin and they were separated at birth. Since you have few ways of establishing the truth about that – birth records, adoption, other secrets like that are virtually impossible to get to the bottom of, even with your hacking skills. The records are, simply most likely not in any database. Your grandparents are both deceased, so you can't verify or discuss this with them. And your dad doesn't have any surviving relatives, besides you."

"Okay,"

Prescott grinned, stared back down at his coffee again. "Except there's one thing that you're forgetting. One very simple yet critical fact."

"What's that?"

"The limp."

Prescott looked up, met Scott's eyes. *The limp.* Of course. His father's distinctive walk due to the unique motorcycle accident that had almost taken his life when he was in his early twenties.

"Yeah. There's the limp. I forgot about that."

"Do you recall the Sherlock Holmes line? The one that states that when you have eliminated the impossible, whatever remains, however improbable, must be the truth?"

"Yes, I do,"

"So there's the possibility that your father had a twin and they were separated at birth. And, however unlikely the case might be, the two men might have, due to living a similar lifestyle — such as the desire to drive fast on motorcycles, had very similar accidents and been injured in alarmingly similar ways. Countless case studies have been done suggested the power that "nature" has in blood relatives who lived separate yet startlingly similar lives — following the same professions, falling in love with similar types of mates, pursuing parallel paths and inborn desires. So it is possible both men had injuries so similar that they'd both walk with the same limp.

"But there's another improbable option that seems far more likely than that."

"And what's that?"

"That your father didn't die on that operating table. That he is still alive. And that the man you saw on the GO station platform was, indeed, your father."

"Doesn't that lead to even further extrapolation and extreme speculation?"

"Under normal circumstances, I'd say yes. But there's something else. Remember, back in high school, you'd relayed to me the fact your mother suspected your father might be having an affair?"

"Yeah, the 'fishing trips.'"

"What might that lead you to think about?"

"That my Dad was living a double life. That perhaps he had another family out there. That could explain his frequent absences."

"But he was never really gone for long periods of time, was he? It was usually weekends or extended trips; a pretty much small percentage of his overall time would have to be with this other family."

"Okay,"

"And, for your father's death to be *faked* so elaborately, that would suggest, at least to me, there are larger forces than a man seeking to abandon one family and spend all his time with another.

"So maybe he was living a double life. Maybe there was an aspect of his life that he kept from you and your mother. Do you remember telling me a bit about your suspicions about something you'd found in your Dad's workshop when you were in University and we used to correspond once in a while? Do you remember telling me about the odd items you'd found in your father's tackle box? You'd described them to me and wondered what they might be."

"Yeah, I remember that."

"Think about the way you'd described those items. What do they make you think of when you're also considering the idea that your father could have been living a double life?"

Scott sipped at his coffee, put the cup down on the table and pursed his lips together.

"James Bond. Secret agent. Those objects looked very much like spy gear. At least, my impression of what spy gear might be."

"Exactly," Prescott said. "It's improbable, but the most likely of all the things we spoke about."

"And it would explain so many of those odd moments, conversations and things about my Dad that I simply didn't understand."

"Still," Scott said, shaking his head. "My Dad. A secret agent? A spy?"

Prescott nodded. "Just think about it."

"But he wasn't in great shape. He had a beer belly, he walked with a limp."

"I'm not suggesting that he was ever involved in high speed car chases, skiing down mountainsides firing ski pole machine gun weapons, scaling skyscrapers and performing Jason Bourne style jujitsu moves. Consider your own skills, abilities and aptitude, Scott. Your father might be a valuable asset more because of his brain, his mind, his ability to blend in and seem unobtrusive."

"Okay," Scott said. "Okay. I get that. And, when you think about how highly Dad regarded his father and how proud he'd been of the fact that he served his country so well, it might make sense."

"Sure. Your father could be operating for CSIS or some other secret government agency, working on something important, something critical."

"Dad did dwell long and hard on the respect for those who put their country's needs ahead of their personal ones, those service people who served their country first; who put the good of our society ahead of their own needs, their own interests. *That* makes complete sense to me."

"So the real question is – what could he have been involved in that was so intense, so top secret, that he had to fake his death and deceive you and your mother in the process?"

Chapter Nineteen

Today

There was, at least according to Scott's interpretation of what he could hear, a single person on the other side of the locked door, trying, unsuccessfully, to get in.

Scott knew, based on the hive mentality of the others he had encountered, that the rest of them; Herb, the security guard, Gary, if he was again awake, and any other employees who had already showed up, would already be aware, through whatever telepathy they employed, of Scott's location; and they would descend upon the locked door and either break it down by sheer force, or perhaps unlock it with the security guard's master key.

So he picked up the metal and plastic chair that was facing the executive desk, and, lifting it over his head, took a deep breath before swinging it in an overhead arc toward the glass.

Geez, he thought as the chair bounced off the glass, leaving a giant spider-web crack on it with a few pieces in the center shattered out completely, leaving a gap in the glass of more than an inch square. *I'd never broken a single pane of glass my entire life. Yet this morning, in the span of less than half an hour, I will have smashed through three windows. And, not only that, but I'm getting damn good at this. I almost smashed through in a single try.*

He threw the chair against the window, breaking through the glass completely. Then he pulled a framed print off the wall and used it to scrape the broken edges from the bottom of the window pane before climbing up onto the window sill and jumping out.

Outside, he found himself in an ally on the east side of the building that led back toward Fraser Avenue.

He ran down the alley, comforted by the simple fact that nobody had either broken or opened the locked office door yet, so, unless somebody was on an upper floor and looking down into this alley, nobody would be able to see which direction he was heading.

His car was parked in a lot of Exhibition Place, a couple of blocks south of the Digi-Life office. It normally took him less than ten minutes to walk between the parking lot and the office, because he cut through parking lots and alleys on his way there.

At the speed he was running, however, he figured he'd be able to get to his car in less than three minutes.

That way he could be in the car, get onto Lakeshore and the eastbound Gardiner Expressway and further away from the people who were pursuing him.

There were very few people on the street as he ran down Fraser, cut across the parking lot of the abandoned old Western Bakery building, crossed Mowat Avenue and got onto Dufferin. The few people he had spotted, the closest one walking at least a block away, from their parked cars to a nearby office building, all seemed to be acting normal, as if this were a morning just like any other – and not one in which everybody had designs to kill Scott Desmond.

That made Scott's theory about the airborne toxin being released inside of Digi-Life's air system seem to hold a bit more weight and also offered him a sense of relief. Now that he was putting more and more distance between himself and the building he could begin to feel a bit better that he would be safe.

A bus pulled out of the TTC station heading back up Dufferin. The bridge itself was still under construction and closed to vehicular traffic, but there was still a pedestrian path allowing foot traffic to cross. Scott raced down the path, passing a middle-aged male jogger in a red and black skin—tight running outfit wearing ear buds.

The jogger nodded at Scott in a single efficient dip of the head.

Normal behavior, Scott was relieved to see, but he still turned his head to ensure the jogger hadn't been tricking him and was actually also turned.

It was nice to bump into someone who wasn't trying to kill him.

Scott was, of course, relieved at the fact the jogger hadn't been turned, as he highly doubted he'd be able to outrun him if the man came after him.

As he got to the far side of the bridge, he could see his silver Mustang parked near the Medieval Times building, and, standing one car over from his own, a blond man in a grey sport jacket. Scott slowed down to a walk, relieved to be so close to getting to his car, so close to escape, but leery about the man who was just standing there.

Scott patted down his front pocket, ensuring his car keys were there, before reaching in and pulling the keys out. Still one hundred meters away from the car he triggered the door unlock function.

Previous to the headlights on Scott's car blinking on and off twice briefly, the man in the gray sports coat had simply looked like he'd happened to be standing there, perhaps having a cigarette before either heading back inside to the Medieval Times building or getting into his car.

But when the lights on Scott's car blinked as Scott unlocked it, the blond man swung his head around quickly, obviously looking to see who had triggered it.

Damn, Scott thought. He's one of them.

When the man turned and spotted Scott, he froze in place, his body became stiff and then he lifted a single arm into the arm and pointed, in that Donald Sutherland *Invasion of the Body Snatchers* manner Scott had become used to.

A fresh chill ran down Scott's spine.

Because of the wind blowing across the bridge Scott couldn't hear what the blond man said as his lips moved, but he didn't need to hear the words to know exactly what the man was uttering.

You won't get away! You cannot evade us!

Chapter Twenty

Two Weeks Ago

Nanotechnology? Nanomedicine? Nanorobotics?

And all of it somehow related to the operating room Scott's father had died in.

It didn't make sense.

Or, at least, it didn't seem to make sense.

Scott started at the computer screen, trying to figure out what, exactly, he'd been looking at.

Scott had spent some time, when he'd initially been exploring investing his father's death, looking at every single person who had been on the chart for being in the operating room during the shift that his father had died, but, often finding nothing of value, had left them aside after a cursory glimpse into his life

Tracking the surgeon himself, Dr. Citino, had revealed the mysterious death which ended up consuming most of Scott's focus. And so, after that, he had pretty much abandoned looking at everyone else who had been there.

After all, Citino had been the one in charge and had also been the one who, like Scott's father, had died under mysterious circumstances.

So there'd had to be something further there.

Scott started exploring the hospital itself, looking for any sort of connection the hospital might have with Ottawa, and he'd been following as many trails as he could. But it wasn't until he started looking further into some of the other staff in the operating room that he found an intriguing yet small connection between Citino and the anesthesiologist, a Dr. Mike Nottoff.

Nottoff had been a research assistant at the Ottawa school where Citino had TA'd.

Deep digging revealed that the two could have possibly met, because Nottoff had taken a course in which Citino had been one of the two team leaders. So, while the records of which TA headed which half of the class, there was at least a fifty-fifty chance that the two of them had met more than once.

It was worth Scott pursuing Nottoff a bit deeper.

He'd found an intriguing series of articles that Nottoff had been a key researcher in.

Several of them had to do with nanotechnology.

In one, research was being done on an area that had been worked on by a team of researchers from Australia and the US, of a nanorobots – the engineering and design of designing devices constructed of molecular components in the scale of a nanometer – searching out and identifying certain proteins and delivering targeted drug delivery.

In another, Nottoff had been a principle investigator in a series of "suicide switch" nanotherapeutic examinations targeting cancer cells – the goal was modeled on the body's own immune system, where white blood cells patrol the bloodstream, and, when detecting specific cells in distress, are able to bind to them and transmit specific signals allowing them to self-destruct.

Scott became fascinated with the detailed research that Nottoff had been a part of, and followed a series of his published papers, despite the challenge he had of properly being able to understand much about it.

Although, when he extrapolated the nanotechnology techniques, particularly the ones in which the nanorobotic device was programmed to seek out particular types of cells and target specific actions on them, it was similar to the manner by which hacking a computer program in order to seek out particular user actions or subroutines might trigger a particular pre-programmed hacked response.

The concepts behind nanotechnology and its use in medicine intrigued Scott.

And Nottoff, who had been a key researcher into that technology, had written or been a key player in the development of no less than half a dozen similar research projects while he was in Ottawa. When he left Ottawa, Nottoff spent a year at University of Alberta's NINT (National Institute for Nanotechnology) before making his way to Laurentian as an anesthesiologist.

It appeared that he had been involved in some sort of research project involving use of nanomedicine in both relaxing and calming techniques as well as in anesthesia. Nottoff had been particularly concerned with producing an anesthetic that would produce no side-effects, such as the nausea or vomiting that was a common result in as many as thirty percent of patients. Nottoff had a single reprimand on his record for engaging in research that involved testing in lab animals that had not been approved by CCAC, the Canadian Council on Animal Care. It was six months after that in which he transferred over to Laurentian.

Scott sat in front of the computer for a long time, considering what he had been looking at.

Had Nottoff used some sort of experimental nanotechnology on Lionel Desmond?

Had it been some sort of experimental anesthetic nanotechnology? Had it been the use of the cancer-cell targeting nanorobots Scott had read about?

In either case, something had gone horribly wrong.

And Scott needed to find out.

He needed to learn more about Nottoff and where, exactly he was now.

He needed to speak with him.

And get to the bottom of this.

Chapter Twenty-One

Today

Not another one!

Scott quickly considered his options. Based on what he understood about these people, there was a telepathic link between them. This meant that Herb, the security guard and any of the others in the Digi-Life building would know exactly where Scott was.

He couldn't run back down the bridge that crossed over top of the Gardiner Expressway and East-West train tracks and into the Liberty Village neighborhood.

They'd know, through the blond man in the gray sports coat, exactly what way he was running, and could head him off.

So Scott ran toward the man who was still standing there, his arm raised, his finger pointed at Scott, decreasing the distance between them from about fifty yards to a mere thirty.

And when he got to the end of the bridge, he darted left, into the Exhibition Place grounds on the opposite side of the road of where the parking lot was and picked up his speed.

Scott ran across the field and the empty plaza of buildings to his left that he had only ever seen active and open during the Canadian National Exhibition, which took place the last couple weeks of August each year. August was still a month away, but already a fleet of metal barricades, all stacked in neat rows, filled half of the park and adjacent parking lot. It took a long time to set up for the annual event that seemed to be the indication that the end of summer was upon the city of Toronto.

As he reached the next parking lot inside the Exhibition grounds, near where the adjacent Gardiner Expressway to the left began rising up out of the ground and became an overhead highway, he chanced a look over his shoulders.

The man in the gray sports coat was running after him. He was still at least one hundred yards away. Despite being winded from already running, Scott had been able to increase the distance between them, which was good. Because Scott had to start slowing down – he couldn't keep the pace. There was stitch in his side, and the flesh wound on the side of his leg where the bullet had grazed him didn't help matters. It was beginning to ache again. So far there hadn't been a significant amount of blood loss, but Scott knew that continuing to hoof it at top speed everywhere wasn't going to help.

He need to get somewhere that he could sit down, rest, check his leg out, and get his head back on straight.

Running and crawling and falling and smashing through windows, constantly on the run and evading the slowly growing horde that was after him was getting to be a bit too much.

To his left, on the other side of the Gardiner Express-way, he could hear, and see, the Eastbound GO train slowing down to pull into the station. It would stop for a couple of minutes and then head deeper into Toronto, bound for Union Station.

Scott tried to calculate how much further he had to run in order to make it to the platform and board the train. He glanced back, seeing the man in the gray sports coat still behind him. Not having gained any ground, but not having lost any either.

He was far enough way that if Scott just made it to the train before the doors closed, the man would not likely make it on himself. And Scott could get away.

He pressed on, doing his best to increase his speed, despite the stitch in his side, despite the throbbing in his leg.

As the Gardiner continued to rise to the full elevation that it maintained on its meandering stroll through down-town Toronto, Scott could clearly see the GO train as it slowed and eventually stopped on its arrival to Exhibition station.

Gray Suit was one hundred yards behind Scott and Scott still had to run at least that far to get to the walkway that led to the station.

As he ran through the third parking lot, this one smell-ing of a strange combination of horse manure and urine – likely both equine and human – he spotted a few parked police cars that were empty. He wondered if he might be able to find a police officer and enlist help, but figured that there wouldn't be enough time to explain himself before Gray Suit arrived.

And, given the manner by which grey suit and the others at Digi-Life were telekinetically connected, there was a good chance they'd be able to come up with a convincing and consistent story that could put any of Scott's bizarre claims spiraling into nothing.

No, he simply couldn't risk it.

The police cars were parked there anyway, as were a few horse trailers attached to Toronto police logo'd trucks. This was a holding or parking area for them, and not an active place that officers were hanging out in anyway.

He raced passed the final section of parking lot and reached the Exhibition station ticket booth area and the gate that led underneath the tracks – that same gate he had raced madly up three years earlier when he'd spotted his father from across the tracks.

He hadn't made it in time that morning.

But he couldn't let that happen today.

Over the track-side speaker system, Scott could hear the following announcement.

"Doors will now be closing. Please stand clear of the yellow platform lines."

"No!" he yelled, and pushed even harder, racing down the sidewalk toward the train platform.

There were a few people scattered about. As he ran, Scott was struck with the sudden notion that perhaps this was a big mistake. Perhaps everybody here was turned and would be able to easily overpower him. Perhaps going towards any crowd was a huge mistake.

But his legs carried him forward; and as he raced past a few people who had left the train, getting off at Exhibition, they looked at him with slightly bemused stares. Being public transit riders, they likely sympathized with the poor guy who was likely about to miss his train. They'd been there, they'd all had days like that where they were just a few seconds from catching their train or their bus.

So they seemed, to Scott, perfectly normal. Not at all one of the pod-people who were after him.

That was a good sign.

He was a few yards from the nearest doorway onto the train when the latest announcement blasted.

"Doors are closing. Please stand clear. Doors are now closing."

Mark Leslie

Chapter Twenty-Two

Twenty Years Earlier

Scott found out that the redhead's name had been Jessica.

He learned that the reason he hadn't seen her before was because she wasn't from the same university. She had attended Concordia and was in town visiting a friend who went to Mohawk.

Jessica had been a friend of a woman named Charlene.

Charlene approached Scott in the library one afternoon about three days later.

"Say," she said, strolling up to where he sat at a cubicle working on algebra problems in a notebook. "Aren't you the head Wilson grind dancer from last Saturday's party?" Scott didn't even realize the sexy hot tall blonde had even been talking to him until she placed a hand on his left shoulder. Hot women simply never spoke to him at all, never mind talk about any sort of party. He had only, after all, ever been to one – that Halloween one.

And, though his room-mates high-fived and fist-bumped him and began to give him the nickname Scotty Grind, Scott knew that would be the last party he would ever attend.

He remembered musing that if this had been some sort of teen movie, he would have latched on to that nickname, become a central figure in the popular scene on campus and demonstrated the underlying message to the movie that being yourself was the coolest thing a person could be. Perhaps he'd grow cocky and change his behavior and attitude, treat the other nerds with disrespect until he one day fell from grace then had to redeem himself both in the eyes of his previous nerdy peers as well as the new cool friends he had made. He would explain that he had fallen trap to being someone or something people wanted him to be, rather than who he was born to be, who he naturally was; that he'd let the popularity and glamour taint his behavior, making him a cruel and mean person, turning his back on those other quiet and socially unskilled losers whom he had walked among most of his life. This would be a speech given in the cafeteria or in a central square of the school and, upon delivering it, everyone would stand quietly while he slipped away to go bury his nose in a book again. Then someone would begin that slow clap which would eventually inspire others to join in – and soon the entire school would be applauding his bravery, the extreme insight he had been able to help them see. And within minutes, the group would hoist him on their soldiers, and this nerd would again become the most popular student in the school – not because of some "cool" thing he'd done at a party, but because he demonstrated that it was cool to be himself. And there would be a montage of cool kids and jocks shaking hands with and laughing with the nerdy kids. Of the hottest girls in the school flirting with the Poindexters. The world would became a better place where everybody appreciated everyone else, begin to roll credits.

This wasn't, of course, a movie.

It was real life.

Scott knew that the nickname would likely last a few weeks, and whenever one of his room-mates used the nickname or mentioned how awesome he'd made the party, Scott simply grinned and slunk back into whatever solo activity he'd been involved with – usually playing a game or working on some sort of program on his computer -- and the whole thing continued to make him uncomfortable.

And now this gorgeous blonde woman, someone who, just last week, would have walked past him and not even taken a second look at Scott even if his hair were on fire, was standing beside him and looking down at him.

Her hand, soft and warm, sent a strange series of tingles through his shoulder and into his chest. It was so exciting that Scott thought he was having either a stroke or a heart-attack.

"Uh," Scott managed to say. "Yeah."

"That was one of the most amazing parties I have ever been to," the blonde woman said. "And everyone knows that you're the guy who started it all; I mean, Wilson was doing his funky chicken thing, but it wasn't until you jumped in and starting grooving with him that it turned into a thing for everyone."

"Uhuh," Scott said, feeling his throat going dry.

"You turned it into the Wilson Grind Dance; and the party into the Grind Party. Everyone's talking about it."

"The Wilson Grind Dance," Scott repeated the words slowly, and he realized that he sounded like a Neanderthal or some sort of Wildman, like Tarzan, who'd been living among the wolves or the apes, slowly learning the language that other humans spoke by carefully repeating phrases and sentences.

"I knew that was you, sugar," the woman said, and the hand on Scott's shoulder slid down to rest on the back of his shoulder blade. "And I just had to say thank you."

"Yeah," Scott said.

"My name's Charlene," she said.

Scott nodded.

"I know your name is Scott. Or Scotty." She giggled. "Scotty Grind. That's what everyone is calling you these days."

"Hmm," Scott mumbled.

"You're not very talkative, are you, Scotty?"

Scott slowly shook his head back and forth. He looked at Charlene's silky blonde hair, at the regal curve of her nose, at the deep blue gorgeous eyes and quickly glanced away. She was hot, absolutely gorgeous. Women like Charlene simply never even looked at guys like Scott. This was bizarre and uncomfortable and he had absolutely no idea what to do.

"That's okay," Charlene purred. "You're not known for being a talker. You're known for your moves."

"My . . ." Scott managed to say, really slowly ". . . moves."

"Anyways," Charlene said, taking her hand off of Scott's shoulder. "The redhead you were dancing with is a friend of mine. Her name is Jessica. She doesn't go to McMaster. She's from Queens. But we're besties. I just came to tell you that she has the hots for you.

Scott blinked at her. "She does?"

"She hasn't said that, but I can tell. She was my best friend all through high school, and we're still tight – we talk and email almost every day. So I can tell. She hasn't said a single thing about you, and she normally doesn't shut up about guys – except for the ones she really has it in for, you know. She gets all nervous and stuff – kind of the way you're acting right now. She pulls her cards up to her chest and doesn't let anyone in; not even me.

"I mean, I've asked her about you, about what you guys said to one another, and she hasn't said a peep, tried to slough it off as nothing. But I can see the longing in her eyes when she mentions you.

"She has the hots for you and she's trying to deny it. But I know."

"You . . . know," Scott said.

"Yeah. So that's why I came over. I figured you should have her phone number and her email." She unfolded a small notebook page and dropped it onto the desk in front of him.

Jessica Stevens
867-555-5309
jessybabe@geemail.com

Scott nodded, his throat now as dry as if Charlene had poured a tall glass of cinnamon into his mouth.

"Call her," Charlene said, and sashayed across the library floor.

Scott watched her and could sense every other guy in the room staring at the display of her hot tight ass swaying back and forth under one of the tightest mini-skirts he had ever seen.

Call her, she'd said.

Scott continued to stare at the doorway where Charlene had exited for at least a full two minutes after she'd gone.

This certainly wasn't a teen movie, and, though he had been the talk of the Halloween party, he certainly didn't know how to embrace this new revelation.

When he stopped staring at the afterimage of Charlene's swaying ass in the doorway to the library, he turned his attention back on the phone number and email address on the desk in front of him.

Chapter Twenty-Three

Today

"*Doors are closing. Please stand clear.*"

"Ahhhh!" Scott yelled, punching his legs down harder and faster than he had ever done before, still a dozen feet from the train as the doors began to close. The flashback to that morning when he'd raced down the platform, seeing his father inside the train as the doors closed just seconds before he got to the train, haunted him.

Not today, he thought, and leapt from the platform and toward the narrowing space between the doors that were closing in from each side.

His right shoulder slammed against the door on the one side and he half-stumbled, half-fell into the train car on his left as the doors sealed shut behind him.

"Geeziz, mister," a young white male with thick beaded dreadlocks who couldn't be more than twenty, had been sitting in the bench seat perpendicular to the doors with his bicycle propped in front of him. "I've never seen anybody so desperate to catch a train. You almost killed yourself getting on."

Scott shook his head, slowly gathered himself to his feet.

"If I missed this train," Scott said looking out the opposite window and spotting Herb and the security guard racing down the platform, "my boss would kill me."

The young man nodded, seeming to be in agreement with Scott; not realizing, of course, that Scott was speaking in the literal sense.

And with that he walked past the young man and headed up the stairs to the mid-level section. Each GO train was divided into a lower section and upper section with two mid-level sections at the front and back of each train, a combination of a landing area with a small section of seats between them. It was on these levels where the doors allowing passengers to pass between train cars were.

As Scott reached the mid-level landing area, he saw Herb standing on the platform and glaring at him. There was a scowl of anger on his face, but still that strange glazed look that had come over him not much more than half an hour earlier. He looked out the opposite window and saw the man in the gray sports coat standing half a dozen yards away on the train platform, glaring at Scott through the window with the same angry look, with that subtle glaze, that Herb had.

As the train pulled away from the station, Scott settled down into a seat in the mid-level section and put his head back for a minute, trying desperately to catch his breath.

He gave himself a minute before pulling off his backpack and pulling out his laptop.

He flipped the top of the laptop open and then dug into the backpack for the hotspot USB stick and stuck it into the side. He waited for the network to pop up then keyed in the passcode allowing him to connect to the cellular network. Within a few seconds he was back online.

His computer was still on the web browser showing Mike Nottoff's research into anesthetic practice to achieve a death meditative state; the process was, essentially, using nanotechnology to produce the same extreme slowing of the heart rate and circular systems that would simulate clinical death while the body lived in in a manner that was not discernable. It was similar to a Tibetan Buddhism practice known as "Death Meditation" where the body can exist in a state that mimics death, preserving the body's skin, organs, and central nervous system.

Could that be what they did with Dad, in order to fake his death?

That certainly made sense.

And there was, as Scott and Mr. Prescott had speculated, some deeper reason as to why it would become necessary to fake Lionel Desmond's death.

Something Scott must have tapped into so deep that someone out there wanted him dead.

He must have been on to something; something so secret, something so powerful, that he had to be stopped.

He was looking at this page when Herb called him into his office.

But, for someone to hack into the air ventilation system of the Digi-Life offices, it couldn't have been just because Scott had discovered this. Someone must have been tracking his research, understanding that he was getting ever closer to the bottom of this; and they'd gone in, some time before today, to set the trap that was launched when Herb first pulled out that gun.

Scott sat staring at the screen, trying to figure out what to do next, where to turn.

He kept thinking back to his conversation at that café with Mr. Prescott.

The man, the first and only mentor Scott had ever had, was a beacon of reason and perhaps the only person Scott figured he could trust.

It was time to call Mr. Prescott.

Scott clicked on the Skype icon on his computer. He could use Skype's phone function to make a call to Prescott and enlist his help in this bizarre mess he found himself at the center of.

The little yellow Contact button indicated a numeral one on an unclicked tab of the left nav bar of Scott's Skype program. He tapped it.

It was Gary.

Thirty seconds ago Gary had keyed in the words: *Are you online?*

The little pencil icon was dancing below those words, indicating that Gary was typing something else

Where are you? Appeared on the screen on the next line.

I stepped out, Scott typed.

What the hell is going on? Can we chat?

The electronic ring-tone indicating that Gary was attempting a video call to Scott sounded.

Scott stared at it, wondering what he should do.

Since Gary couldn't reach through the screen and strangle Scott, he figured he should see what was going on.

"Scott? What the hell happened? Where are you?" Gary was sitting at his desk in the office in his little sanctum sanatorium on the second floor. "The last thing I remember, we were standing in the kitchen and I was wondering what the hell you seemed so worried about. Then it's black. I have no idea what happened. I woke up with a massive headache laying on the floor in the nurse's station just a few minutes ago. All I can remember is chatting with you in the kitchen. But when I woke up, you were nowhere to be found.

"Scott – what the hell is going on? What happened to me? Where the hell are you?"

Gary seemed genuinely confused. Scott wasn't sure what to say to him.

"Scott. Answer me, buddy. I'm scared."

"I'm not sure what's going on, Gary." Scott said quietly. "But you need to get out of the building. But before you leave your desk area, hold your breath, man. Hold your breath and get the hell outside as quickly as you can."

"What the hell?"

"Just do it, Gary. I don't have time to explain. I've got another call I need to make. Just hold your breath and get out. If you can, avoid every single person you spot, stay as far away from them as possible. Try not to let anybody stop you. Just get out of the building as quickly as you can."

Scott pressed the hang-up icon on Skype and then toggled over to a browser where he'd stored Dr. Prescott's number.

He had to call the man, try to figure out his next move.

He found the number and then toggled back to Skype and keyed the number in to the digital numeric pad there.

It began to ring.

And ring.

And ring once more.

Then it went to voice mail.

"Mr. Prescott. Tim. It's Scott Desmond. I need you to contact me. My mobile phone is dead, so I'm not sure how you can reach me, other than Skype." He proceeded to leave his Skype dial-in number for Mr. Prescott, then hung up.

The little yellow icon indicated that Gary was texting Scott again.

Then a second numeral popped up.

Someone else was trying to reach him.

Scott clicked on the button. Saw it was a new contact request – this time from Mr. Prescott – it was combined with an incoming video call.

Scott accepted the video call and Prescott's face appeared on the screen.

Scott knew, immediately, that there was something wrong. He could see it in the glazed look on his old teacher's face.

"Don't say it, don't say it," Scott whispered under his breath.

But, as he fully expected, he knew. It was too late. They had gotten to Prescott. They had infected him as well.

"You won't get away!" Prescott said. "You cannot evade us!"

Scott tilted his head back, closing his eyes. And, just as he did, he noticed three train ticket checkers wandering down the lower section, checking for people's tickets.

Damn, he thought, realizing he didn't have a ticket. Although, what would be the worst thing that could happen? They'd toss him off the train once they arrived at the next stop, which was Union, which was where Scott had planned on getting off at anyway.

He sat and watched them make their way through the crowd. There were three ticket cops. Two of them were questioning people and asking to see their tickets or proof of purchase, and the third one, a short female with straight long hair tied into a pony tail, was making her way down the aisle when she looked up at Scott.

She made eye contact with him and then started walking toward him quickly, ignoring all the other passengers who were sitting in the rows she passed, some of them holding out their proof of purchase.

But she was oblivious to their gestures.

She was purposefully stalking her way toward Scott.

And she had that vacant, haunted glazed look on her face.

Mark Leslie

Chapter Twenty-Four

Twenty Years Earlier

Scott called Jessica the next day.

He left a message.

The first one was simple, and part of a script he had actually taken the time to write out because he hadn't been sure what to say to her. So it worked out really well; particularly since the script was more of a short speech anyway – conversation, particularly conversation with pretty girls, was not something that came easy to him, or even at all, really.

Conversation, unlike computer code, had too many variables, too many unwritten, unspoken nuances that were impossible to control and prepare for.

She when he got Jessica's voicemail message of "This is Jessy. Can't speak now, so lemme know what you got, sugar," he consulted his script and mostly stuck to it, except for the fact this his verbal delivery was a little bit stunted and broken; not as slick and smooth as the words he had carefully composed.

"Hi Jessica. This is Scott Desmond. From the party. The Halloween party. I got your number from your friend Charlene. And I just wanted to call to let you know that I had a really great time. Er, thanks."

That had gone okay. A simple message. But then, as he sat there, he realized that he hadn't left his phone number, so how could she call him back?

So he dialed the number again. He had to leave his phone number.

It rang three times then went to her voice mail.

"Hi Jessica. It's Scott again. I, uh, just left you a message. It's Scott, from the party. Uh, I'm, uh, Grind Dance guy. From this past weekend. So, uh, I got your number from Charlene and she said I should call you. So, I'm, uh, calling you. Hi. The party was pretty cool, wasn't it? I had fun. I really had a lot of fun. And I liked you. Er, I liked dancing with you. So I'm calling. Okay. Bye."

Shit! He thought. *What the hell was that? I had fun. I liked you. I liked dancing with you. What an idiot.* Not only that, but he'd forgotten to leave his phone number. Idiot.

So he called back a third time.

"Hi Jessica. It's Scott, from the party. The dancing party. Anyways, I just left a couple of messages, but realize that I forgot to leave my phone number so you could call me back. I'd love to hear from you. So please call me back. My number is 867-555-3878. That's my number. So now you have it. So now you know how to contact me. At my number. Okay. Bye."

About fifteen minutes later, after spending the entire time staring at the phone and nervously thinking back to the words he had spoken on the last message, Scott called back again.

"Hi Jessica. It's Scott from the party. I was worried that I left the wrong number. I can't remember if I said "38" or

"83" – I sometimes get those numbers confused. So my number is 867-555-3878. Three. Eight. Seven. Eight. Not Eight, Three. Okay, thanks."

He let almost half an hour pass before he called again.

"Hi Jessica. It's Scott. From the party. I left my number, 867-555-3878. I kept thinking, because I still get it wrong, that I might have not told you the correct number. So I thought I'd call again and make sure I did it right this time. I really like you. I had a fun time at the party. Dancing with you was fun. Call me, okay? 867-555-3878."

When more than an hour had passed and Scott hadn't heard back from Jessica, he became really nervous.

He had really liked her.

And he must have blown it.

I'm coming off too aloof, he'd thought. *Too cool.* They had, after all ground into one another, kissed, gazed into each other's eyes, and pretty much made love, though it was with all their clothes on. But they'd both orgasmed. They'd shared something truly intimate. And here Scott was leaving simple messages telling her to call him.

Sure, he'd said he liked her. But he also said he'd liked dancing. He needed her to know that he really liked her; that he was really into her. That he wanted to see her again.

Scott remembered hearing a song by Billy Joel on the radio called "Tell Her About It" – he didn't realize, particularly since he'd never been in a relationship, that this was a song meant for a guy who tended to keep his emotions and deeper feelings to himself and was potentially pushing away his girlfriend by not letting her know his feelings, but not opening his heart to her. Since Scott had never been in a relationship, he didn't understand those dynamics. So he took the song to mean that a guy could win a girl over by expressing his deepest feelings to her. As Joel sang, he had to tell her everything he felt and *give her every reason to accept that you're for real.* He had to let her know he needed her. He had to let her know how much he cared.

It went even further downhill from there.

"Hi Jessica," he said to her voice mail box. "It's Scott. From the party. I've left you a few messages and I think I've made a stupid mistake. You see, I'm trying really hard to act all cool and confident. But that's just not me. I'm not a cool guy. I'm pretty quiet and I don't party much. I don't party at all, in fact. The Halloween party was my first time. I've never kissed a girl before. You were my first. And, I've never made love before, either. You were my first. Not that we had sex. But we did, sort of. It was really hot. But not just hot; I felt something. I felt close to you. I felt like we had something special. And I don't want to lose that. I don't want to lose you. I told you that night that you were the most beautiful thing that I have ever seen. And I mean that. You are amazing, gorgeous. I had been admiring you all night. It wasn't just the dancing, the grinding. I felt we had a thing long before that, when I'd been watching you earlier that night. You're a beautiful woman, Jessica . . . Jessybaby . . . that's what your email address is. Jessybaby. Can I call you that? Can I call you my Jessybaby? Anyways, you're a beautiful woman,

Jessybaby, and I want to make you mine. So please, call me when you get a chance."

He hung up, feeling good about it. Sure, he had left a series of silly messages. But this time he laid his heart out on the line, told her everything that he'd felt. Billy Joel would have been proud of him.

Billy Joel might have also suggested there was such a thing as coming on too strong too quickly. He might have cautioned Scott about just how easy it is to scare a woman away with coming on way too strong and with obsessive behavior.

But Billy Joel didn't know Scott.

Scott didn't have any mentors or any role models who had shared any sort of woman advice with him.

So he left three more extended voice mails like the last one; and he would have left more if he hadn't heard the robotic voice from her cellphone company announcing that her mailbox was full.

That's when he turned to email, and composed a more than five hundred word detailed outline of all that he felt for her.

She didn't email back.

He called again later that day, but her voicemail was still full.

So he followed up with another email twice as long.

And the day after that, he forwarded both messages to her, worried that she hadn't received either one, because she never emailed back. She never called, either.

Ever.

Chapter Twenty-Five

Today

Scott slammed his laptop closed, wondering if the air supply on the GO train could have been infected with the same airborne contaminant that had affected the Digi-Life building.

No, he figured, taking a quick look around at everybody else on the train, including the other by-law officers. That couldn't be it. Nobody else on the train that he could see was behaving out of the ordinary.

Well, no more than the way people tend to behave in that fidgety "I'm not guilty" manner when a bylaw enforcement officer was checking for tickets, or the way that people tend to sit up a bit straighter and put both hands on the wheel when their vehicle comes into proximity with a police cruiser on the road.

So the good news was that this hadn't become a train filled with a mob of zombies out to get Scott.

No, it was just the single officer, and she was striding purposefully toward him.

Scott slipped his laptop into his bag, hopped out of the seat and proceeded to head to the back of the train, slid the heavy door opened and stepped out into the enclosed section where the trains connected. Despite being fully enclosed it was louder and breezier in that small three foot by three foot space. Looking through the window into the next car, he couldn't see any bylaw officers there, and so he pulled that door open and stepped into the car.

Then he quickly walked across the mid-level section and down the flight of five stairs to the lower section. He could hear the door separating the cars slide open behind him, and he rushed a little more quickly down the center aisle across the train.

As he reached the bottom of the stairs at the other side, he glanced back and saw the bylaw officer heading down the aisle. She was gaining on him. He hoofed it up the stairs and down the mid-level aisle toward the next set of connecting doors.

This time he moved through them quickly, not pausing to see if there was anybody on the other side before opening the doors to the next car.

He rushed inside, then down the stairs and along the lower-level aisle again, picking up speed.

As he raced up the stairs, he could tell that he had gained a few feet on his pursuit from the officer, as she was just rushing down the stairs on the opposite side as he was rushing up on his side.

He moved more quickly through the mid-level area, through the passageway connected to the next train, and through the next car. This time, he was already at the next set of doors when he could see, looking along the upper section, that she was just coming through the doors on the far side.

Good. He was still gaining.

He went through the next set of doors to the following car, and then the one after that.

It was feeling good. He was evading her. He only hoped that he would be able to stay ahead of her long enough for the train to stop at Union Station and he could rush off.

Except, he figured his luck wasn't going to hold up.

Because as he rushed up the last set of stairs, instead of an entranceway connecting to another car, it was a car with a conductor booth on it; one of those cars in which there was a conductor to operate the train when it was heading in the opposite direction of where the engine was.

"Oh shit!" Scott said, stopping in his tracks.

He turned, spotted the officer across the opposite side coming in through the opposite doorway and heading purposefully toward him.

"So much for my great lead," he gulped, standing there and feeling a cold sweat trickle down his face.

Mark Leslie

Chapter Twenty-Six

Twenty Years Earlier

Scott's father only spoke to him once about girls.

And, by the time he had, it had been far too late.

Scott had, of course, already done the damage, already not only pushed Jessica away in a maximum overdrive sort of way, but had, most likely frightened the poor girl into thinking that he was going to end up stalking her for the rest of her life.

The ill-timed chat about girls had come on the same day Lionel Desmond had woken Scott with that alarming prick, the accidental poppy stabbing. Scott still wondered at just how the poppy could sink in so deep and cause such a painful stab.

He remembered rubbing his shoulder that afternoon when he and his father had been in the boat.

Lionel Desmond, normally quiet and pensive and not a man of many words when they were out on the boat, could sense that something was wrong in his son, and so asked.

Scott told him the whole story. Okay, not everything; he kept some of the heavier petting details about the party, the groping and feeling up and, especially, the orgasm out of the tale. He relayed the tale as if Jessica had been a girl he had danced a lot with that night, that they had kissed, and that he later found out had liked him.

Then, feeling proud of himself and the manner by which he had interpreted the Billy Joel wisdom from that song, he'd explained to his father how he had laid it all out on the line with Jessica.

He would never forget the look of horror on his father's face when he went on to explain the repeated voice mail messages and the things he had said to her in his emails. And the worse part about it was that Scott didn't tell his father about all of it, he held back most of the details, making it sound like he'd just left a handful of voice mails and a couple of emails.

But still, his father had been horrified.

And he gently explained to Scott how coming on strong was one of the worst things that a guy could do.

"But I've seen the shows and hear it in songs," Scott said in frustration. "Women want men to talk to them, to be honest, to share their feelings,"

"They do," Lionel said. "But that's only *after* they're already a couple, already together, already committed."

Lionel explained how women seemed to be more attracted to men who kept to themselves, who held back, played their cards close to their chest.

"I don't know," Lionel explained. "Maybe they see men as projects, as a challenge, as something to work at."

Lionel went on to explain to his son how he and Lionel's mother had gotten together. How Lionel had been infatuated with Janelle, but how she barely noticed him no matter what he'd done. How she hadn't started paying attention to him until he had started dating her cousin. "That was when I knew," Lionel had said. "That's when I figured out that she must really like me. So I kept dating her cousin, because I wanted to make sure she was really falling for me."

Scott was initially confused, but then, when he started to put the pieces together at the complexity of the relationships between men and women, when he started to map out the counter-intuitive push/pull behavior, thinking about it like the way that magnets repelled one another when you pushed both north ends together, but how they came together when you flipped the north and south ends, it all started to make sense.

Relationships could follow set patterns, they could be mapped and planned and figured out.

So Scott figured, were he ever interested in pursuing a relationship again, he would be able to, like his father, manipulate the situation to create the optimal setting for a girl to fall for him.

But he didn't want just any girl.

He wanted Jessica.

And he knew, beyond a shadow of a doubt, that he had blown it big time; he had messed it up in such a complete shit-bomb way, that there would never be any going back.

And that hurt tremendously.

It dug deep to the bone.

It was devastating to even think about her. So he couldn't imagine ever falling for anyone again.

It simply hurt too much.

So he tucked away the information that his father had shared, the wonderfully deceptive manner by which you could manipulate someone into doing things, into falling for you. The way you could trick someone into falling in love with you.

Scott not only learned the folly of his ways with Jessica, but was startled to learn just how deceptive and manipulative his father could be.

Chapter Twenty-Seven

Today

Scott watched the top of the officer's head on the opposite side of the train as she moved forward through the doorway connecting the two trains. He stood rooted in his spot, at a dead end, having run out of trains to escape through.

When her head bobbed out of view as she ducked off to her left to take the short flight of stairs to the lower section and head in his direction, Scott shot forward and raced up the stairs to the upper section.

He only hoped that his footfalls weren't so loud that she could hear him crossing over-top of her. He figured the ambient noise of the train and the low rumble of conversation of the commuters might be enough to keep her from hearing him.

He made it to the other side and raced down the stairs and toward the door to go back into the car they had both just run through. When he looked back he could see her on the mid-level on the opposite side, standing in front of the engineer's booth. She hadn't yet turned around, but would likely figure out which way he had gone. There was, after all, only a single possible path he could have taken.

Scott rushed through the doors connecting the trains and then proceeded to race back through in the opposite direction.

As he rushed he glanced out the window trying to determine, based on the scenery, just how far the train was from Union Station. He spotted the base of the CN Tower and knew they were pretty close. Just a few minutes. He could even feel the train beginning to slow down in its approach to its final stop on the morning's commute.

He figured, with the number of cars he had, he might just make it, so long as he didn't bump into the other by-law enforcement officers.

He had wondered if they might also be turned; but he figured they couldn't have been – otherwise they would have, in tune with the female officer pursuing him, have joined in the chase, knowing exactly where she was, and, via her understanding, where he was.

If they had been turned, the three officers could have easily cornered him.

He felt pretty lucky, and, as he raced, speculated about how she could have been infected if it hadn't been an airborne agent in the train's ventilation system. She must have been infected earlier. How, Scott couldn't figure out.

He had to get away, get off this train, to a secure location, so that he could figure things out.

He just needed more than a few minutes to compose the elements that he knew and try to make heads or tails of the situation; why these people – both the people that he knew as well as perfect strangers, had been consumed with the desire to stop him, to kill him. And, more importantly, who or what was behind all of this?

And, as he ran through another car, continuing to be pleased that he hadn't yet bumped into the other bylaw officers, and seeing that the train was now entering the tunnel at Union Station, he was thinking he would get that chance. It was likely less than a minute or a minute and a half before the train would stop, the doors would open, and Scott could rush out.

But his luck ran out.

As he was just about to open the doors that would take him onto the next train, he could see, through the glass of the two door windows, one of the other by-law enforcement officers standing in the next car on the mid-level and writing up a ticket for a commuter on that level.

"Shit!" Scott said, turning to look back. On the opposite side of the car, the female officer was coming through the doors.

Mark Leslie

Chapter Twenty-Eight

Four Days Ago

Scott finally managed to track down Nottoff, and had gone as far as driving up to Sudbury to meet up with him.

He had located the man's phone number, finally, after several hours of digging and searching. The number was unlisted and not in any of the crack-able lists he had access to.

It was even blocked in the hospital record system, in a scramble-code encryption that Scott had never seen before, and never would have expected in simple internal hospital emergency contact information that was already behind a tight firewall.

So when he finally deciphered the scramble-code encryption – a task that took almost a full week of tinkering – he was startled to get a "this phone number is not in service" message.

"Damn!" he'd said, slamming the phone down after the third attempt to call the number.

He knew, then, that he would need to head north and meeting Nottoff face to face.

He'd managed to swing getting the Friday off from work, despite being under a tight deadline at Digi-Life, so he could make the trek up north to meet Nottoff. He'd done so by spending most of the evening the Thursday night working late on the project. Not that he didn't already work late most evenings during this challenge – with looming deadlines, it was easy to still be in the Digi-Life offices until eight or nine at night.

But this time, he stayed there until eleven-thirty, taking care of some of the tasks that he normally would have put off until Friday.

It was a four hour drive north to Sudbury from Toronto; a trip that Scott had become proficient at. He planned on making the best use of the extra work he'd had to put in at Digi-Life and buffering that with the best time of day for making such a trip with a guaranteed time for the lightest possible traffic.

He figured if he went to sleep for a few hours, slept from midnight until three in the morning he could drive north up Highway 400 to Sudbury and be there by seven Friday morning when Nottoff would be getting off shift, according to the schedule.

The highway would be virtually dead that time of night, so Scott would be able to make good time heading north.

And he'd arrive in time to intercept Nottoff after his shift.

It would all work out well.

And it had been working out well.

Until he got about forty minutes north of Barrie, on a lonely and quiet stretch of Highway 400.

That's when his front passenger tire blew.

It happened suddenly.

First, the tire gauge on his dashboard lit up, informing him that he had low tire pressure. He'd seen that before and knew, based on the sensitivity of this alarm, he could drive for several days before having to actually check the tires.

But not this time.

The low tire gauge went on, and then, within seconds, there was a loud thrump-thrump sound coming from under his car, and the vehicle rocked up and down as if it had one of those hydraulic shocks you'd sometimes see on muscle cars. The car lurched forward and began to slow.

"Holy shit!" Scott muttered, navigating the car over to the side of the road.

He didn't even need to apply the brakes. Taking his foot off the gas petal combined with the additional friction of riding right on his right front rim slowed him down quiet enough.

After fiddling with the spare tire from the trunk for about five minutes, Scott knew he wasn't going to be able to fix the flat himself.

So he called the Automobile Association emergency number, told them of his situation and explained where he was, approximately, on the highway.

The dispatcher informed him that the closest contractor was about forty minutes away, but that they'd be there as quickly as possible, and retrieved his cell phone number so the driver could contact him in case there were any issues with locating him. Then she gave him her name

(Jeanette) and a confirmation of his request number. 3Q547

The highway was pretty desolate and only ran north and south. Scott wondered how it would be possible for anybody driving on this highway *not* to see him. But he kept that observation and those thoughts to himself.

He needed the service guy to come, fix his flat tire for him, and then get going.

This was going to set back his plans big time.

Fifty minutes later, ten minutes after the time quoted to him, when he tried calling the Automobile Association again, he got stuck in a "we are experiencing a significant volume of calls right now" message reminding him his call was important and he was in a queue, to stay on the line for the next available operator. The repeated message included the fact that if this were an actual emergency, requiring medical assistance, to hang up and call 9-1-1.

He stayed on hold like that for another half hour, before he thought of pulling out his laptop and seeing if he could locate the contractor vehicle's location himself.

He used the hotspot option from his mobile device to connect to the internet, and within minutes was inside the Automobile Association's internal servers, browsing through the calls made within Ontario.

There was nothing in the system indicating that he had called at all. His Automobile Association customer number showed that the last time Scott had made any sort of service call had been three years earlier, when he needed a battery boost on a cold February morning. There were no other calls registered since then.

A search of the first name (Jeanette) or the confirmation number for his call 3Q547, revealed nothing either.

It was as if Scott had never called.

Ten minutes later, a trucker pulled over about twenty yards ahead of where Scott was parked. In the time he'd been sitting there, a little over half a dozen vehicles and two large transport trucks had all shot past him on the highway. None of them had even slowed down when they passed him, but several had moved over to the far left lane either in order to leave additional space, or perhaps because they were worried about "catching" whatever had caused this poor sucker to have to pull over.

The trucker lurched out of his truck and walked over to see Scott.

"Car trouble?" he asked in a southern drawl that Scott seemed to think might be Louisianan.

"Yeah," he said. "Flat tire."

"You got a spare?"

"Yeah. I'm just, ah, not all that good at it."

"It'll be my pleasure to help you," the trucker said. "The name's Pete."

"I'm Scott."

Pete stuck out his hand, shook Scott's. "Pleased to meet you, Scott. Now let's see what we can do to help you out here."

Scott was back on the road and drove no more than twenty minutes before the "hill assist" light flashed on his dashboard. The tire pressure gauge went off again, and so did the low fluid indicator. The dashboard lit up like one of those musically synced Clark Griswold styled houses in those YouTube videos, lights blinking on and off, flashing at different speeds, with beeps and boops and buzzes popping into the night air.

He pulled over to the side of the road.

This time, instead of calling the Automobile Association, he simply hacked into their servers again, and registered his location, the fact that he needed a tow, and, instead of entering his own Automobile Association number, he entered that of a fellow member whose information he could easily see now that he was hacked in.

The contractor arrived within ten minutes. At that point, as the vehicle was pulling in behind him, Scott went back in and revised the number to his own.

The driver towed him back down to Barrie where, by the time all was said and done, it was morning and the service station was already open.

"We have no idea what happened to your vehicle," the service manager, obviously confused, said to him after his team had spent about twenty minutes with the car in the shop.

"The entire electrical system is compromised and throwing errors we have never seen before."

Scott sighed, wondering how he could have such bad luck.

But he knew better.

He was on to something here. And somebody had hacked into the Automobile Association, to prevent him from ever getting his call.

They had, obviously, also hacked into his car's computer system as well.

Someone was trying to prevent him from heading north to see Nottoff.

Someone was on to him

Because he must have finally been on to something.

Mark Leslie

Chapter Twenty-Nine

Today

Scott watched the brunette bylaw officer stalk toward him from the opposite side. Her eyes met his and he felt a cold dread in the pit of his stomach.

"Shit!" he said again, glancing back at the officer writing the ticket on the connecting car.

The train hadn't yet stopped at the station yet, and Scott knew there was no way that it would and the doors would be open before she got to him.

"Looks like somebody is going to be paying the piper," a middle-aged woman with her hair tied up into a little bun at the back of the top of her hair said to him over-top of the paperback she'd been reading.

Scott was prepared and fully expecting to hear her utter *You won't get away. You cannot evade us*, in that monotonous drone he had heard all too often that morning, but she just tsked a couple of times and shook her head at him.

That's when Scott looked past her to the yellow and orange emergency clasp on the GO train window.

"Excuse me," he said, pushing passed the woman and pulled at the large emergency handle with his right hand while pushing at the bottom of the window with his left.

It was heavy, but, by design, the window tumbled out and smashed onto the tracks and platform below.

If only the other windows I'd gone through earlier today could have been this easy, Scott thought as he stood on the vacant seat beside the bewildered woman who was still shaking her head, as if, instead of vandalizing the train he had just cut a raunchy fart.

Ducking and putting his left foot onto the window ledge, Scott pushed himself through the window and leapt down to the train platform. Even though the train had been moving at a considerably slower speed than just a minute earlier as it continued decelerating into Union Station, it was still high enough and fast enough for the additional forward momentum to pitch Scott off of his feet.

He rolled forward over his shoulder to help break the fall and felt something plastic and metallic crunch under his back as he completed his roll.

My laptop, he thought.

First his cellphone and now his laptop!

Scott, being such a savvy purveyor of technology, thought it was interesting that his great strengths were the things that were compromised; losing these computerized devices might have been the equivalent of Samson losing his hair, Thor losing his hammer, or Iron Man losing the power source in his specially designed suit.

He didn't have time to worry about that, of course, because he was running for his life. But the computer, the mobile phone, those were the ways Scott had to connect to the internet, to do the research he needed to do, to be able to hack into the systems and find answers.

He knew he was close, really close.

That must be why these people were after him.

The only question was: who were they, and, since that's the way Scott's mind worked, how were they able to do this? How were they able to take control of people using that airborne agent?

Without a computer, where and how would he be able to pull this off? His first thought would, of course, have been to contact Mr. Prescott, his trusted computer mentor – certainly the man would have some decent computers and a Wi-Fi connection in his home – but they'd taken over Prescott's mind and body, so he had to rule that out. The Toronto Public Library, perhaps, with their row after row of free computer and internet access?

Maybe.

But first, he needed to get away from them, get to a safe spot.

All of this went through Scott's mind in the matter of a couple of seconds. By the end of those thoughts, he was already back on his feet and starting to race down the platform toward the stairs that led down into the depths of Union Station.

The platform was already filled with commuters, several of them standing and looking aghast at the man who had leapt from the window of a moving GO train. He heard a few *Are you okay, buddy*'s as he got to his feet, heard a few other NSFW exclamations; but nobody, of course, reached out to him.

You simply didn't reach out like that – not in downtown Toronto, anyway. If this were rural Nova Scotia, or a really small town in Ontario, the inclination would be to see if the stranger needed help. But here, particularly during the morning rush hour, the mentality was more *Oh, God, what now?* Combined with *How is this going to delay me getting to where I need to go?* rather than any sort of actual concern for another.

The platform wasn't as full as Scott had seen it – since the train he had arrived on hadn't completely arrived, only about half of the station platform was full. On the opposite side of the platform another train sat there with its doors open. Most of the occupants had gotten off and other commuters were now getting on.

There were small groups of people standing on the train platform on the side Scott's train was coming in, aligned approximately with where they knew the doors on each side of each train car would be at when the train came to a complete stop.

It's amazing how much people were creatures of habit. Scott imagined that the majority of the people he saw standing in those spots, stood in those exact same spots at the exact same time every single working day that they went to work or school or wherever their daily commute brought them.

Humans were, in many ways, as predictable as computer programs.

That thought made Scott consider something regarding the people who were able to take over his boss and colleagues from work. It could, perhaps, be easily done when you knew a person's routine – when you knew exactly where they would be.

Of course, tracking people using their unique mobile device was easy enough to do. Entire traffic update apps relied on the constant stream of vehicular commuters who were in traffic; the speed of the highway based on a constant flow of updates about location.

Scott wondered if perhaps the fact that his cell phone had been crushed and broken relatively early in his flight for safety might have actually been beneficial.

Being the hacker that he was, he had provided a mod to his mobile phone that scrambled the signal, sent conflicting reports of GPS location – except at such times when he required accurate GPS location in his phone for particular apps. He thus has built a toggle switch into the program; so that when he required GPS tracking use, he could easily turn it on and off. But, considering that a program is only as good as its' weakest line of code, it was possible that someone out there could hack into it, and be able to track where he was, even with the GPS scrambled.

Thus, having the phone break might have been a good thing after all. If they had been tracking him based on the GPS signal from his phone, at least they no longer had that.

As Scott moved down the platform, he found there wasn't enough space to run. The crowd had come to a funnel section, and, with a mass of bodies all trying to get into the narrow space of the stairway, where there was room for no more than two people side by side descending the stairs together (and good luck to anybody on their way UP that stairwell, because the mass of people moving down would overtake them – they'd be like a stick thrown into a fast moving river), the crowd came to a virtual stop.

The train car Scott had been on passed where he was standing, and he'd briefly spotted the female ticket officer glaring at him through the window; the angry look on her face which was, as Scott knew it would be, layered with that distinctive glaze he had noticed in every single person who had been converted into the single-minded horde.

Scott stood at the back of the crowd and watched, in horror, as the train completed its stop at the station. The car he had been on stopped just on the other side of the stairwell entrance he was trying to get to. He considered bolting backwards and turned, but a throng of people that went on for more than a dozen feet had already moved in behind him, with more people heading his way, and the crowd, still at least twenty feet from the narrow stairwell entrance, was inching its way forward.

He debated whether it would be quicker to get into the stairwell or to fight his way backwards through the crowd, and figured his best move might be to keep going forward, see if he could lose himself in the crowd.

As the group of bodies shifted forward, Scott kept one eye on the train car the officer had been in and continued to glare warily at the people around him.

While most of them had the typical ten-foot commuter stare glaze, none of them appeared to have the zombie-glaze he had already gotten pretty good at identifying.

No, this crowd was tuned-out of most of their immediate surroundings, barely acknowledging the others around them – they were moving with a slow purpose, to their destination, most of them barely in the moment, with ear buds and noise-cancelling headphones on their heads. Several of them had taken up the familiar head down and glancing into their palm stance as they read email, checked the Facebook or Twitter stream, read text messages or were perhaps consulting their GPS to ensure they were heading in the right location.

The crowd poured out of the train Scott had arrived on, and several dozen people from the adjacent train car added to the molasses-like crowd that was slowly moving to the stairs.

About ten feet away, to the left of the stairwell entrance and on the other side of the wall that covered the stairway, Scott spotted the glazed face of the GO train bylaw officer. She was focused on him and moving forward.

A quick calculation of Scott's speed heading toward the stairway entrance and the distance left to go, compared with her distance from the entrance and the speed the crowd she was in was moving was favorable toward Scott winning. She was, after all, moving through a much narrower area, and the group she was with was merging into the mainstream crowd already there – so, though she was a third closer to the entrance, she was moving at about half the speed Rob was.

He would just make it, so long as things continued to move the way they were.

Scott kept a wary eye on her the whole time, and then noticed her right arm come up and, holding something that he couldn't see in her hand, reached forward and pushed against the back of the neck of an older gentleman in front of her. It was a syringe, Scott realized, based on the way in which she held her hand.

The old man exclaim in a surprised yelp of pain, and turned his head about, as if to see who had dared do that to him.

But after a couple of seconds, his head swiveled toward Scott.

His face, previously one that had worn the standard zombie commuter look, now bore the distinctive glassy-eyed glaze much like the bylaw officer.

So it wasn't just an airborne agent. There was a way of injecting the toxin into someone's bloodstream as well.

Scott continued to inch forward, watching as the bylaw officer deftly handed the syringe to the older man over his shoulder. He didn't even look back to see where she was handing it – he obviously knew exact where she was handing the syringe and took it in a manner much more smooth than any pair of relay racers handing off a baton.

The older gentleman shifted the syringe from his left hand to his right and then proceeded to inject it into the neck of the woman in front of him.

"Dammit," Scott said, realizing that, in such a crowd, so long as the fluid in the syringe didn't run out, this entire mass of people could be converted, and he was in huge trouble.

Scott forced his way ahead of the young woman and the middle-aged man in front of him, rudely pushing them both aside. Then he muscled his way past an older lady. He couldn't afford anything other than brute force to get through this crowd more quickly. And he didn't have time to look back to see who else had been converted.

He just kept shoving and moving forward. People exclaimed and swore at him, but, so far, nobody shoved back or tried to stop him. Best of all, no cold hand of one of the mob that was after him came down on his shoulder announcing that he was caught, announcing in no uncertain terms that he would not get away that he could not evade them.

Within a few more seconds, he was in the stairwell, and continued to shove past people, doing his best to get yet another body between himself and the growing group of people coming after him. The only person on the stairs who shoved back was a white hippy college-aged young man with thick black dreadlocks. "Chill, man!" the young man said, and gave Scott a rough shove back.

Scott moved quickly passed the hippy and heard him continue to curse at him.

When he finally got to the bottom of the stairwell, the crowd fanned out again into the basement hallway and Scott was able to bolt ahead, begin to actually walk with some speed.

He headed off to the left, darting around people, getting past them, and putting more bodies between himself and the pursuing group whose number he couldn't be sure of now.

As he moved, he glanced back, noticed the distinctive glaze about fifteen feet back of the bylaw officer, the older gentleman, the middle-aged woman and one other person, the white hippy college student with thick black dreadlocks who had shoved back. He now wore the glazed look on his face. The student was at the front of the pack and he was moving more quickly than any of the others.

Scott pushed past a few more people and started to run.

He tore off down a hallway on the right, a direction that most of the crowd was not heading in, and proceeded to a set of double doors that led to a series of underground tunnels that ran under the city – figuring he might stand a better chance if he kept moving through the underground systems, considering the likeliness of security monitoring cameras on the street above.

He raced down several corridors, most of the crowd thinned out behind him. But the bylaw officer, the hippy and the middle-aged woman were all still just a few yards behind him, keeping at the same distance with every corner and short set of stairs that he ran.

The older man was no longer pursuing him – Scott figured he was somewhere behind but just couldn't keep up with the rest of them.

Not that it mattered. There were already three of them in pursuit. He only hoped he didn't run into anyone coming back the other way. After all, he had no idea where Herb or the Digi-Life security guard were, nor the man Scott had left behind at Exhibition station. But there were all somehow connected; they knew what the others knew. It wouldn't be hard, even if only a single one of them had eyes on Scott, for the others to know, and be able to intercept him.

When he spotted a pair of elevator doors in the basement of the hotel lobby ahead, he ran toward them, seeing that the call button, lit up, had already been pressed, even though nobody was standing there – it had likely been pushed by someone who, impatient, likely went over to the entrance to the stairway just a few feet away. It was likely someone who wanted to move from this pathway and up to the lobby a single floor up. Scott was continually fascinated with just how lazy the average person could be – although, in this case, the frustration with waiting had overtaken the inherit laziness.

But he wasn't going to complain – because it could just work out for him.

If he could get inside and take it to another floor, he'd be out of eyeshot of them, at least for a few seconds. But that could be enough to finally allow him to slip away, try to prevent someone from intercepting him.

The timing was almost perfect as the elevator pinged that it had arrived at this basement floor just as Scott was running up to it.

Mark Leslie

He'd be able to slip inside, jab at the DOOR CLOSE button and be hidden.

As the elevator door slid open, Scott was shocked to suddenly be standing face to face with his father.

Standing quietly inside the elevator, Lionel Desmond glared at his son, a serious and stern look on his face, and raised his left arm to point a gun directly at Scott's head.

Chapter Thirty

Twenty-Seven Years Earlier

"*There are more things in heaven and earth than are dreamt of in your philosophies,*" Mr. Prescott said, standing in front of Scott's desk. "That's a line from Shakespeare. *Hamlet*, in fact."

Scott nodded, looking confusedly at his mentor. The two had been working together for several weeks now. Scott spent many lunch hours in the computer lab, working on various programs and trying to solve particular issues related to running out of memory on the systems he was trying to program.

"It's not behaving as expected," Scott said. "It just doesn't work this way." Scott had said. "What does that have to do with *Hamlet*?" Scott had no use for, no time for literature or fictional characters – they had no bearing on what was important to him, no bearing on computer programs.

"Prince Hamlet was expounding on the fact that, despite all of the things that we know, there are often things beyond that we can understand or even perceive.

"He spoke that line to his friend Horatio when they were speaking about the rumors of Hamlet's father, the

King, being spotted walking around, in ghost form, some-time after his death. They were debating the existence of ghosts when Hamlet suggested this."

"Okay, sure," Scott said. "Whatever. But what does that have to do with programming?"

"Do you remember the psychology program we worked on last week?"

Prescott was referring to the special intricacies of how to program a simple Artificial Intelligence subroutine that mimicked human conversation; in this particular case, the human question and answer rhythm of a therapist speaking with a patient.

The subroutine began with a statement introducing itself as a doctor and then asked the user to type in their name.

The user would type in their name, and the program would return with. "Pleased to meet you, X." – inserting whatever the user typed as their name into the X variant.

Then, the computer would say: "So, X, tell me how you are feeling today?"

When they used typed in a phrase, the computer would repeat it back. For example, if the user types in "blue" then the computer's response would be: "What do you think might be making you feel blue today, X?"

The conversation went on in that similar fashion, with the program set to look for certain keywords in the response and, based on detection of particular phrases, it would respond with various lines. It made it appear, to the average user that the computer was actually attending to what the user was saying and responding genuinely and in an unscripted fashion.

"Sure, I remember that."

"What did you learn from working on a program like that?"

"That you could fake a real-life conversation using a set of pre-programmed routines, scripts, and keyword indicators."

"Exactly. What else can you intuit from that?"

Scott caught on. "That some things aren't exactly what they seem."

"Bingo!" Mr. Prescott said, his index finger thrust into the air. "And that, my young friend, is precisely what is happening to you right now."

"But there's no program running," Scott said. "I've stopped the program and I've run the script to see the lines of text; I've made modifications to particular lines and I've re-run it."

"Yes," Prescott said. "Or so you thought. Maybe this program was set to trick you into thinking that you *had* stopped the program, when, in fact, you had done no such thing. What if all of the commands you typed were within the still-running program, and not at the code level you thought? What if the program was designed to make you *think* that you had hacked into it when, in fact, you hadn't and were still working through a pre-programmed routine?"

Scott slowly nodded his head and a giant grin spread on his face.

"That," he said. "Is deceptively crafty; absolutely marvelous."

And then he set about to try to actually stop the program itself. For real this time.

Chapter Thirty-One

Today

"Dad!" Scott yelled.

"Hi Son," Lionel replied, nodding his head. "Duck!" He raised the gun a little bit higher as Scott instinctively followed his father's advice and dipped his head down between his shoulder blades while bending his knees.

His father stepped forward, out of the elevator and produced, seemingly from nowhere, a thin plastic novelty clown mask that he slipped onto his face, while leveling gun in front of him with his left hand.

Scott stepped forward and to the side, turning to watch what his father was doing.

Lionel Desmond pulled the trigger and, instead of a gunshot, Scott heard a static-sounding electrical hiss and saw something shoot out of the front of the gun like Spider-Man's webbing shooting from his palm, or, perhaps more accurately, some sort of wired hook from a gun on Batman's utility belt.

The mechanism shot out and struck the hippy full in the chest and an additional electrical buzz shot through the air. The hippy dropped to the floor, immediately unconscious. The wire shot back to the gun. Lionel quickly pocketed the gun with his left hand and switched hands that were holding the mask to his face while his right hand simultaneously pulled something out of his breast pocket that looked like a lipstick tube.

He aimed the lipstick tube at the bylaw officer, pressed a button, and a blue flash of light shot out from it, striking her in the chest. She reacted in the same way as the hippy, and, twitching on the spot for a second, dropped to the corridor floor.

Lionel Desmond then pocketed the lipstick tube and stepped forward, intercepting the middle aged woman who was running closer. She reached out for him. "Surrender Desmond to us!" she said, in that deep robotic voice Scott had started to recognize and hate.

Scott's father moved forward as if to take her in the warm impassioned embrace that two long-lost friends might display when seeing one another in an airport terminal. But, as she moved in, he twisted around, held her in a half-nelson move by thrusting his arm up and through hers, forcing her neck down. Then he twisted and her head fell forward and she crumbled to the floor.

"Did you break her neck?" Scott asked, watching her fall.

"No," Lionel said. "Sleeper move. She's alive. Just out cold. Let's go."

Lionel shoved his son all the way into the elevator and stepped inside to join him.

He immediately thumbed the DOOR CLOSE button, poked the button for the top floor, the eighteenth and turned to face his son as the doors whooshed close.

"I knew you were still alive," Scott said quietly.

"I saw the conviction in your eyes that day, Scott. I was afraid that you'd keep pushing, that you'd dig and uncover what was going on."

"What is going on, Dad? How is it that you're alive?"

"Long story," Lionel said. "Let me see your bag for a second."

Scott handed his father the backpack. Lionel took a small flat black plastic object about half of the size of a smart-phone from his jacket pocket and ran it over the bag. The object beeped quietly in three short tones and a green led light on the top of it flashed.

"Okay," he said. "It's clean. There are no tracer bugs in it." He looked at Scott again. "How about your phone?"

"It's dead."

"We still need to toss it. Even when non-operational, some of the GPS functionality can still be there."

"Okay," Scott pulled the mobile phone out of his pocket and held it up to his father.

Lionel took the phone, looked up at the ceiling of the elevator and then pointed up. "Give me a boost, would you?"

Scott locked his fingers together and Lionel placed a foot into his son's make-shift step, pulling himself up with his right hand on the wall. Once he got up about a foot, he popped the drop ceiling tile to the elevator open and slipped the cell phone in. The tile settled back down and he said. "Okay, let me down."

Scott did so.

Lionel then hit the button for the fourteenth floor. The elevator stopped at that floor. "C'mon," he said, stepping out of the elevator.

They stepped out and the elevator resumed its ascent empty.

"Stairs," Lionel said, heading down the hall and beckoning for his son to follow. "Let's go."

They were moving too quickly, even with his father's debilitating lurch, to really speak. They were both enough out of breath that it made conversation difficult. And every time Scott did try to say something – he had a thousand questions after all – his father held up a single finger to his lips.

"Let's get away, make sure we're safe, and I'll answer all your questions. Okay?"

"Okay."

The proceeded down the stairwell for six full flights and came out into the hallway on the eighth floor. Lionel led his son to the left down the corridor, over to a spot that contained a walk-way connecting two of the buildings at an upper level. They then ran down another couple of flights before getting to the sixth floor of the second building where they went back into the hallway and this time caught an elevator on its way down to the lobby on the ground floor.

They cut through the lobby then crossed the street, went in through the main doors of a hotel lobby, then cut out the side door, crossed the side street, went East until they were on Yonge Street and they took a cab six blocks north, where they got out, Lionel Desmond paying cash with a ten for a six dollar fare, but not bothering to ask for any change or a receipt.

They crossed the street, went through another hotel lobby, slipped in to the hotel restaurant, then, at the end of the hallway that led to the restrooms, they slipped out the emergency exit, raced down the alley and jumped onto a streetcar on King Street heading West. Whenever Scott tried to say something, his father repeated the gesture of placing a finger in front of his lips.

They got off the streetcar just a few blocks later, at the corner of King and Peter, and walked back to the hotel there, went in the side door of the lobby and stepped inside the elevator where Lionel hit the button for the tenth floor.

When Scott opened his mouth and attempted to say something his father merely said. "This is our last stop, son. Once we get to our room I'll tell you everything. I promise."

They got off on the tenth floor and took a left down the hallway to a room. Lionel produced a card, unlocked the door and they went inside. It was a large room with two double beds and a roomy sitting area with a small sofa and an armchair.

Once the door was closed, Lionel guided them over to the sitting area, waited for Scott to sit down and said: "You've got a million questions. Which one can I answer first?"

Scott sat there, stunned. He did have a million questions. So many things to ask. But, ever the pragmatist, he figured he'd start with the first.

Mark Leslie

"How are you still alive?"

Chapter Thirty-Two

Today

"How am I still alive?" Lionel Desmond said. "It's a long story, son. So let me take it back a bit. I know enough about your investigation into my death to determine you know I wasn't always out on fishing trips all those times."

"No. I figured out that much. You're working for CSIS or some government group like that, aren't you?"

"Something like that," Scott's father said. "It's a secret group. A spin-off of CSIS. We work collaboratively in unison with an offshoot of the CIA in the US."

"Holy shit. What's the name of the group called? How long has it been around?"

Lionel Desmond looked down at the floor and pursed his lips together. "I have been cleared to let you know the type of work that I do, particularly since your investigation, if it continues, could compromise the security of this operation. But I'm not authorized to explain further details about the group I work for."

"But I have been very careful, Dad. I haven't left any trail, any breadcrumbs."

"I know. You've done very well, Chief, and I'm proud of you."

Scott couldn't help but feel a warm glow at those words. It had been ages since he'd heard his father utter anything like that. And he couldn't be sure if it was the pride his father expressed or just the fact he called him "Chief" just like he used to when Scott was young.

"How did you get started working for this group, Dad?"

"It related to my own father; but I can't get into that right now. There isn't time. There's a lot that's more pressing that I need to explain to you in a very short time."

"Why?"

"Because I need you to understand this quickly and make a decision right now."

"About what?"

"When the group I work for began following your investigation, they knew you would keep hacking until you found something. And you were getting close. Really close. In fact," Lionel continued. "Your adept investigation techniques and hacking skills are what led me to convince them that you should join me."

"Join you?"

"Yes. Fight the good fight alongside me."

"Hold on, Dad. Back up for a second. This is all coming too fast."

"It'll continue to come fast, son. There's a lot more. So, please, just give me a few minutes to lay it out as quickly as possible. Let's back it up for a minute, okay?"

"Back it up? Sure. Can we start with you explaining why you're not dead? Why your death was faked the way that it was?"

"Yeah," Lionel said, pinching the bridge of his nose between his fingers as if staving off a migraine. "I was going to explain that. It wasn't easy to do, but it was my only choice. You and Mom were in jeopardy if they thought I was still alive. You see, I knew too much. "

"About what?"

"About a top secret security project. A project run by a small faction of the secret offshoot of CSIS. A group that became convinced of their own power, their own invincibility, their own belief that they knew better, had the answers, and could take control. Few people knew about this group that was going rogue. But I found out about it, and I protested. So they needed to get rid of me."

Scott got up and walked over to the window.

Lionel stood up, maneuvered in front of his son and closed the blinds. "Stay away from the windows, son. As far as they are concerned, you're dead now, too."

"What?"

"Please," Lionel said. "Sit down and listen. Just listen."

Scott did what his father said and Lionel paced back and forth, consulted his watch, then looked at his son.

"Okay. Let me try again."

"I have been working on projects related to the national security of Canada and the United States. As I mentioned, I learned something I wasn't supposed to learn.

"Do you recall the G20 Summit in Toronto the summer of 2010? Do you remember the violence that happened in the clashes between the protesters and the police? The innocent people who were brutalized, the millions of dollars in damage to businesses and personal property?"

Scott nodded, struggling hard to stay silent as he listened.

"Notoff's research in nanotechnology led to an incredible find. He learned how he could inject micro-bacterial elements into the bloodstream that would trigger something in the innate fight or flight instinct in humans. Instead of engaging "fight or flight" it triggered surrender. Complete and full surrender.

"The effect was what riot police had been looking for when they used chlorobenzylidene, or tear gas. It was as efficient, but could be introduced through airborne agents or via injection, very quickly.

"Notoff's research, stuff that was completely stripped from medical records, related to how one side effect of this reaction made subjects entirely complacent with external commands.

"Those side effects led to mind control."

Lionel's phone hummed, announcing a text message and he looked down at it for a quick second. "I've got a minute to tell them if you're in or not. If you decide you want this, there'll be two bodies found in the alley at the bottom of that eighteenth story building from an accidental fall. They will be identified as you and the unknown stranger who assisted you on the elevator – a fictitious vigilante agent named Tom who supposedly disappeared into hiding about six months ago."

Scott nodded that he understood. "Keep going."

"The mind control was consistently pervasive. Notoff later learned how to use nanobots injected into the blood stream to send messages directly to the brain; with the right number of trained operatives, a whole army of people could be controlled in a hive-mind manner.

"When I found out about their plans it I spoke out against it. My role, after all, had always been about preserving and protecting the liberties and freedom of citizens. A weapon like this, it stripped away liberties, it took freedoms away. I hated it from the moment I first learned about it.

"That's why they wanted me dead, out of the picture. That was something I could deal with. But the threats from these people started to come against you and against Mom. That's the only thing that kept me from speaking. But the underlying threat was still there.

"So I had no choice. My death had to be faked so they would stop worrying about what I might do. Hidden, I could continue to watch and monitor, to try to infiltrate them and eventually take them down.

"Only, you spotted me that one day. And your insatiable curiosity led you to continue to uncover things. I knew there was no stopping you, which is why I convinced them. I knew . . ."

Lionel's phone hummed again. He looked down at it, tilted it forward.

"Time's up," he said. "I need your answer. Are you in?"

Scott considered the life he had been living, the solitude, the lack of friends, the absence of any sort of meaningful long term relationship. He lived the idea type of life to easily slip away from, leaving virtually nothing behind. Unlike his father, there was no family that would mourn him. For him it was an easy question to answer.

Mark Leslie

Scott nodded. "You don't even need to ask. Of course I'm in, Dad."

"Good," Lionel said, thumbing a quick reply into his phone. "Good," he said a second time, this time letting out a long slow breath.

Scott stood, put his hand out toward his father. He father looked at his hand, looked back up at him and then pulled him into a tight embrace. Scott couldn't remember the last time his father had hugged him; all he knew is that it felt good.

He had been alone for such a long time.

But not anymore.

He not only had a purpose, a skill he could put to good use to serve his country, just like his father and his grandfather, but he was given a second chance to be with his Dad, to learn from him, to fight alongside him.

"Dad?" Scott said over his father's shoulder. "You know I'm in. One hundred percent right?"

"Right."

"But let's say that I refused to help, to join you, to join the cause. Let's say that I wanted to go back to my life, walk away from this."

His father hugged him tighter, the pressure almost cracking Scott's ribs. "There is no going back, son. I don't want to dwell on that."

"I figured as much," Scott said, barely grunting out the words from the tightness of his father's hug. "But, out of curiosity, if I said no, and needed to be taken care of, how were you going to do it?"

Scott could feel his father shaking his head as he let out a short laugh. "I always loved the fact that you weren't ever afraid to ask the hard questions."

They both shared a nervous laugh, neither wanting to think too long about what that horrid possibility meant.

Finally, Lionel pulled back and placed his hands on either side of his son's shoulders, giving him one last quick squeeze. "Okay," he said. "Time to get moving. We have a shitload of work to do."

"Together," Scott said.

"Together," his father agreed.

ABOUT THE AUTHOR

Mark and his father, Eugene (late 1990s)

Mark Leslie is a writer, editor and bookseller from Hamilton, Ontario. He has edited **North of Infinity II**, **Campus Chills**, and **Tesseracts Sixteen: Parnassus Unbound.** Mark's books include **One Hand Screaming**, **I, Death**, **Haunted Hamilton**, **Spooky Sudbury** and **Tomes of Terror**. His website is www.markleslie.ca

31980069R00143

Made in the USA
Charleston, SC
04 August 2014